P9-CRL-107

STAR WARS®
THE WRATH OF
DARTH MAUL

STAR.WARS®
THE WRATH OF
DARTH MAUL

BY RYDER WINDHAM

SCHOLASTIC INC.

New York   Toronto   London   Auckland   Sydney   Mexico City   New Delhi   Hong Kong

www.starwars.com
www.scholastic.com

No part of this publication may be reproduced, stored in a retrieval system, or transmitted in any form or by any means, electronic, mechanical, photocopying, recording, or otherwise, without written permission of the publisher. For information regarding permission, write to Scholastic Inc., 557 Broadway, New York, NY 10012.

ISBN 978-0-545-38327-1
ISBN 978-0-545-43367-9

© 2012 by Lucasfilm Ltd. & ™. All rights reserved. Used under authorization.

SCHOLASTIC and associated logos are trademarks and/or registered trademarks of Scholastic Inc.

12 11 10 9 8 7 6 5 4 3 2 1   12 13 14 15 16 17/0

Cover illustrations by Mike Butkus
Printed in the U.S.A.   23
First printing, January 2012

For Allan Kausch, who introduced me to Darth Maul

TABLE OF CONTENTS

PROLOGUE

The prong-nosed rat knew that the dark heap lying in the tunnel was a dead man. He could tell by the incredible stench. Unable to detect any other predators in the tunnel, the rat's sharp nose twitched with excitement at his discovery, a large and easy meal, all for him.

The rat edged along the side of the tunnel, stepping over the skeletons of other creatures — many small skeletons, but others quite large — as it moved toward the corpse. Ragged scraps of broad, waterproof fabric were piled over the lower half of the dead man's body. His head, arms, and chest were exposed. A fine layer of dust covered his skin, barely concealing the bold, jagged tattoos that adorned his remains. His head rested at an odd angle against the ground because of the long, sharp horns that jutted from his skull. The rat slunk closer to the body and opened his jaws.

The rat never saw the fist that crashed down on the back of his neck. And then the man, who was very much alive, opened his yellow eyes as he rolled over and lashed out with his other hand to seize his prey. He kicked away the fabric scraps he'd been using as blankets, revealing the mechanical apparatus that formed his lower body.

The apparatus was affixed to the man's midriff, just below his rib cage, and consisted of a droid carriage equipped with six metal legs. The legs were unevenly jointed, cannibalized from the parts of ruined droids, each leg ending with a tapered point. As the prong-nosed rat writhed in his clutches, the man skittered out from under the blankets like a monstrous robotic spider, his metal legs clacking against the tunnel floor.

He had no recollection of how he'd lost his lower body or who had grafted his torso to the droid carriage. Although he knew the tunnels that had become his domain, he did not know that he was on a planet named Lotho Minor. Nor did he remember his own name. And for the moment he didn't care. His mind was on only one thing.

Food.

He tore into the rat and began eating it greedily. A few minutes later, as he licked the last of the gore from his lips, a familiar feeling returned to him. It was the only feeling he had, the only emotion he knew when he wasn't delirious with hunger. Hatred. Not just anger and rage, but pure and total hatred.

He hated his circumstances. Hated the tunnels and

all the vermin that ventured into them. Hated being hungry, and being unable to rest without some other creature trying to take a bite out of him. Hated that he knew all those distractions were meaningless. The primary object of his hatred was something far more significant, something he despised with such incredible intensity that he . . .

Can't remember.

Hated his bad memory too.

How had he arrived at this place? How long had he been living like a wild animal? His yellow eyes darted back and forth, sweeping the tunnel as if he might find a helpful answer in the shadowy nooks, amidst the gnawed bones of small creatures that littered the ground.

Nothing.

He grimaced. He wanted to remember. He wanted to know.

The frustration was like a painful itch that he knew he could never ever scratch. He lowered one hand to his side, and his fingertips brushed against one of his cold metal legs.

Wasn't always . . . like this.

He knew that he wasn't a man anymore, that he hadn't been one for years. He was just a creature in a filthy tunnel. And then he remembered the object of his hatred.

A man . . . the man who left me for dead.

The hatred surged through his veins, filling him with

the urge to kill anything within reach. He surveyed the skeletons and rotting carcasses on the tunnel's floor, then used his droid legs to launch several swift and vicious kicks that sent bones crashing against the walls. Finding a large rib cage, he seized it and brought it down hard across the back of one metal leg, then threw aside the splintered bones. He found no satisfaction in this petty destruction. He only hated more.

Why can't I remember?!

Balling his hands into tight fists, he felt his sharp, dirty fingernails dig into the bases of his leathery palms. He gnashed his teeth and squeezed his eyes shut as he struggled to conjure up a memory, any memory, that would help him recall his own identity.

It was then, while he felt his hatred burning within, that a spark ignited in his mind. And he saw a sea of fire. . . .

CHAPTER ONE

The cater

The boy named Maul had to stand on his tiptoes to peer through the thick window in his small room. The window was polarized to block heat and light, but the view was still so intense that it made the boy squint. The light did not come from the sky, which was choked with black, smoky clouds, but radiated from the river of lava that flowed below the facility where Maul lived. Turning his head slightly, he saw the lava empty into what looked like a wide, fiery sea.

The planet's name was Mustafar, according to the droid that looked after Maul. The droid also served as the boy's teacher and had shown him holograms that illustrated Mustafar's terrain and the planet's location in the galaxy. The droid had shown him holograms of other worlds too. Maul had a hard time understanding that the holograms represented actual planets, but he had to memorize their names and correctly indicate their locations or the droid would subject him to a painful shock.

Fortunately, Maul was alone. Looking through the window, he tried to spot any signs of life. Occasionally, he would glimpse Mustafar's armored natives riding lava fleas in the distance, heading for the northern region where they worked as miners. A few times, he had even seen ore haulers traveling across the sky. At the moment, he could not see any Mustafarians or vessels, just the never-ending flow of lava, fire, smoke, and clouds.

The droid had told Maul that he wouldn't last long on Mustafar's surface, but that didn't stop him from wanting to venture outside. After all, if the Mustafarians could move about freely, why couldn't he? He might need Mustafarian armor to protect him from the heat, and also some kind of breathing apparatus. He wondered how difficult it would be to acquire such things. He had no reason to believe a Mustafarian would just give him what he needed to survive. But he did imagine that going outside would be exciting.

Maul moved slightly and saw something shift across the window's surface. Maul realized it was his own reflection. He could see only the top of his head, which had multiple small horns. Like the rest of his body, his head was distinguished by red and black patterns. His eyes were bright yellow with small black pupils.

The first time he had seen his reflection, he had been startled, because he had thought he was seeing another person. For all he knew, his reflection *was* another person, another boy who looked like him and echoed his every movement. A boy who was semitransparent, suspended in the smoky air outside the room. A boy who was free to roam the planet's volcanic surface without fear of injury, who could leave Mustafar and go anywhere he wanted. A boy who could help Maul escape.

Maul wished he were that boy.

Bracing his hands against the seamless area where the smooth metal wall met the glass, Maul jumped up so he could see more of his thin body reflected in the window. He jumped again and again, fascinated by his leaping reflection as well as the sound of his bare feet smacking against the metal floor. He pushed himself away from the window as he jumped back, still facing the window, and continued jumping for several minutes. He didn't stop until well after his breathing had become short, his feet had gotten sore, and his leg muscles had begun stinging with pain.

Catching his breath, he turned away from the window and surveyed his room. The room's only remarkable features were a single door against the wall opposite the window and a cold-water faucet that was operated by a palm sensor, positioned over a small drainage hole in one corner. The door was made of thick metal, the same material as the walls, floor, and ceiling. The bottom of the door had a narrow horizontal slot, through which the droid would sometimes shove a small tray of food, usually bits of uncooked meat. Maul could not see through the slot, because it remained sealed when not in use, by a sliding sheet of metal. Above the door was a convex blister that housed an audio speaker and also a photo-receptor, which allowed the droid to watch Maul at all times. There weren't any controls to open the door from inside Maul's room, at least none that Maul had ever been able to find.

A chime sounded from the speaker, alerting Maul to begin his exercises. Even though his room was not very large and his legs were still tired from jumping, he knew better than to ignore the chime. He immediately began running in place.

At first, Maul kept his arms tucked by his sides. Then he started pumping his arms up and down to match the steady rhythm of his leg muscles. He wanted to close his eyes and pretend that he was somewhere else, perhaps a larger room, but he was not allowed to close his eyes while exercising. He forced his eyelids to stay open and pumped his legs faster.

The chime sounded again. Maul stopped running, fell back against the floor, and began doing a series of sit-ups and leg lifts. After several minutes, the chime sounded, and Maul rolled over to do his push-up exercises, alternating between one- and two-handed push-ups. Several more minutes passed before the chime sounded again, signaling the exercise session's end. Maul collapsed against the cold floor.

Someone's coming.

Maul pushed himself up and stared hard at the door.

Although he could not hear approaching footsteps, he knew the door would open in a moment, and a visitor would be standing in the chamber outside. He didn't know how he knew this. He just knew.

Maul could imagine only two possible visitors. One was the droid that looked after him. The other was the Man, who rarely visited. The Man wore a dark robe with a deep hood that left most of his features in shadow. Maul had never actually seen the Man's eyes.

Maul hated the Man even more than he hated the droid. The Man frightened him.

The door made a hissing sound as it slid up and vanished into a slot in the ceiling. Standing outside the doorway was the droid. Made of shiny black metal, the droid had a bulbous head with five red mechanical eyes called photoreceptors and a mesh-grille vocabulator for speaking, and a cylindrical torso that held four long, jointed pincers for arms. The torso rested on a swivel-hinged abdomen that had six spiderlike legs.

Maul never knew what to expect from the droid. Sometimes it brought food or medicine or sprayed Maul with antiseptic cleansers or escorted him to a larger adjoining chamber where it would chase him or let him run in circles. Other times, it would talk to him and teach him words.

Usually, the droid brought pain.

Once, the droid had delivered a bright green and yellow snake that wasted no time in attacking Maul, sinking its venomous fangs deep into the boy's arm. Maul screamed and then threw his own body down on top of the snake's to crush it. As ravenous as he was enraged, Maul had not been able to resist taking several large bites of the dead snake, which had been more than his small stomach could handle. After that incident, the droid had returned with medicine, bandages, and a stomach pump.

Now, standing before Maul in the doorway, the droid slowly extended one pincer away from its body and swiveled the tip in a broad circular movement. Maul kept his eyes focused on the rotating pincer as he felt his muscles tense, bracing himself to leap away from it. He didn't notice the small panel that opened below one of the droid's eyes. The opened panel exposed a socket that housed a telescopic arm tipped with a hypodermic needle. The arm lashed out, jabbed the needle into Maul's right shoulder, and then rapidly retracted into the droid's head. The droid had taken just a fraction of a second to make the injection — so little time that Maul barely comprehended that the needle had pierced his skin.

Maul blinked as he reached up and rubbed his shoulder. He realized that the droid had done something to him and had rotated its pincer only to distract him. And then he felt a strange, warm sensation spreading throughout his body. He frowned at the droid, and then his eyelids drooped and his legs buckled. The droid's arms extended, catching the boy before he could hit the floor.

The spider-legged droid picked up the unconscious boy and carried him out of the little room without any difficulty. The boy was not at all heavy. He was barely three years old.

When Maul awoke, he was lying on a metal bench in a large high-ceilinged chamber that he had never visited before. Three tall, narrow windows were set into one wall, illuminating the floor in front of Maul but leaving most of the chamber in darkness. Through the windows, he saw molten rock cascading past a black jagged cliff.

Maul did not remember falling asleep or leaving his own room. He suspected he was about to be disciplined. He wondered if he hadn't done all his exercises correctly or if he had made some other mistake. Not that it mattered. Sometimes he was disciplined without any explanation at all. He had been learning discipline since he had learned how to walk. One of the first things he learned was not to cry. Crying never made anything better. Crying only made things worse.

Maul slowly pushed himself up from the bench. He felt cool air against his back and suspected there was a vent or a doorway behind him. Looking around the chamber, he noticed five red lights glowing in the darkness of one nearby corner. He recognized the lights as the eyes of the spider-legged droid.

Maul rubbed his right shoulder. He remembered that the droid had struck him in the shoulder earlier, and suspected that the droid had made him fall asleep. He wondered what the droid might do next. Would it kill him?

The droid lurched out of the corner. Maul hit the floor with his bare feet, and began running as fast as his small legs could carry him away from the droid. Staying out of the light that stretched from the windows across the floor, he darted toward an inner wall, heading for the source of the draft he'd felt against his back. His vision adjusted to the darkness and he found a quadrangular doorway. He did not hesitate to run through it, even though he had no idea of what awaited him in the next chamber.

Darkness. A chamber without windows. Then he glimpsed a dim sliver of light ahead. Ignoring the droid's clattering footsteps behind him, he ran toward the light, which emanated from somewhere beyond a curved wall. He knew he couldn't outrun the droid, but he didn't dare stop.

Maul ran around the curved wall and entered a long, narrow corridor. Illuminated by small rectangular lamps embedded in the walls, the corridor was so long that he couldn't see the other end. Maul kept running. He heard the droid's footsteps pause at the corridor's entrance. He hoped the droid was too large to follow him into the corridor.

Risking a backward glance, he saw the droid had already tilted its body sideways so four of its legs tapped against the wall while the remaining two continued to scramble up the floor, propelling its metal body after Maul. Maul gasped as he turned his gaze forward, never breaking his stride.

He heard the droid's footsteps grow louder and knew it was gaining on him. He somehow sensed the droid was about to snare him with a pincer. Desperate and determined to evade the droid, Maul jumped to the side, planting one foot against the wall to his right, then sprang to the opposite wall, keeping his feet moving so that he traveled two steps across the vertical surface in a diagonal descent to the floor. Maul heard the pincer slam into the floor behind him, and he jumped up to make two more quick strides along the right wall before he flung himself back to the floor, still running forward. As he ran, he heard a loud and satisfying crash from behind, and he knew that the droid had tripped over its own legs in its failed effort to keep up with him.

Suspecting that the droid would not only recover but also be very angry with him, Maul ran faster. His heart was pounding as he saw that the corridor terminated at another quadrangular doorway. He exited the corridor fast and arrived in a chamber that was unlike any place he had ever imagined.

Broad tapestries hung from the walls, which were also decorated with strange sculptures. Carved furniture, made from strangely jointed and highly polished bones, rested on a wide rug that had once been an animal's hide. At the chamber's center, an enormous orb of transparent greenish blue liquid, nearly two meters in diameter, was suspended in the air above a circular dining table. Dozens of small, multicolored aquatic creatures swam within the orb, some so close to the surface that their swishing tails sent ripples around the orb's circumference.

Maul was so amazed by all the wondrous things in the room that he almost forgot that he had stopped running. He just stood there, looking from the swimming creatures to the decorations. But as he studied the carved furniture, he instinctively realized the chamber was a special place. It was a place where someone sat and looked at all the things in the room. It was a place where someone lived. He knew the droid did not require such luxuries. He was certain that this place was the Man's lair.

"Welcome, Maul," rasped a low voice from behind Maul. "I have been expecting you."

Maul froze at the sound of the Man's voice. He locked his eyes on the floating orb. He wished he could become invisible.

"I *had* expected that the droid would lead you here," the unseen Man continued. "The way you ran along the walls to evade the droid was *most* impressive. But then you always have been a clever boy."

Maul had heard the Man talk like this before.

Compliments were almost always followed by punishments. Maul braced himself as he kept his eyes fixed on the floating orb. As unnerved as he was by the Man's presence, he was more fascinated by the aquatic creatures inside the orb. He wondered if the creatures were edible.

A screech of metal sounded from the doorway that Maul had just entered, and the droid pushed its body out of the narrow corridor to emerge inside the chamber. After the droid righted itself so that all its legs touched the floor, it moved up beside Maul, stopping short of the animal-hide rug. Maul shifted his gaze from the floating orb to the droid and noticed two of its legs were now bent at odd angles. The droid swiveled its mechanical eyes to stare at Maul and said in a droning tone, "You should not have run away."

"Leave us," the Man snapped at the droid.

The droid tottered away from Maul, moving toward a wide doorway on the other side of the room. Maul wanted to leave with the droid, but instead he looked at the floating orb and remained where he stood.

"You may face me," the Man said soothingly.

More than ever, Maul wished he were the free-floating boy who appeared to exist beyond the window in his own room. He tried very hard not to tremble as he slowly turned and looked up to face the Man.

As usual, the Man was wearing his dark robe with the deep hood, but he had pushed the hood back so it was draped behind his head. Maul was surprised to see his exposed face. The Man had blue eyes, fair skin of a singular color, and a head of wavy hair. Maul was also taken aback by how different the Man's head was from his own. The Man didn't even have horns.

The Man lifted his eyebrows as he looked at Maul skeptically. "You can talk, can't you?"

Maul nodded.

"Yes?"

"Yes," Maul replied.

"You will address me as Master Sidious."

"Yes, Master Sidious."

Sidious smiled. "Excellent." He stepped past the boy and stopped beside the floating orb. Maul noticed that all the aquatic creatures within the orb swam to the far side, putting distance between themselves and Sidious. Sidious glanced at the creatures as if he found them only mildly interesting. "Maul, I have something important to tell you. I want you to listen carefully."

Maul listened.

Speaking slowly, Sidious said, "You . . . are . . . remarkable." Looking away from the watery orb, he faced Maul and added, "Very remarkable."

Maul did not know why he might be considered remarkable, or how Sidious expected him to respond. He decided to remain silent.

"Our galaxy is home to trillions of life-forms. Some are large, others small. But as diverse as they are, the truth is that most life-forms are just like these fish." Sidious gestured at the fish with a dismissive wave, and the fish appeared to shiver within the orb. "They seldom stray far from where they were born. They spend their time worrying about their next meal, about how they might avoid pain, and how long they might live. They live in fear of one another. And then, they die. It does not matter if they are an insect, a fish, a man, or . . . a snake."

Once again, Maul thought of the snake he had been forced to kill.

"You have already traveled great distances," Sidious continued. "You may have been born on the planet Iridonia, but you came to my attention on another world, Dathomir. There, the females rule and enslave the males. You were just an infant, and yet the most powerful beings on Dathomir were afraid of you. They wanted you dead because you were different." Sidious smiled. "Do you know what makes you so remarkable, Maul? So different from ordinary life-forms?"

Maul shook his head and answered meekly, "No."

Sidious raised his eyebrows slightly and pursed his lips. Shaking his head, he said, "That is not the correct response. The correct response is 'No, Master Sidious.'"

Maul swallowed hard, then said, "No, Master Sidious."

Sidious smiled again. "You are different because you are stronger. You have powers. You know things

17

in advance. You look at the closed door to your room, and you know it is about to open. You have fast reflexes. Others only dream of anticipating moments as you do, or being able to move so fast. In this way, you and I are alike, Maul, except that my powers are much greater. My powers are greater because I know many things that you have yet to learn, such as how to make your powers work for you. Do you understand?"

"Yes, Master Sidious."

"Good. Good." Sidious walked around the watery orb until it was positioned between him and Maul. From Maul's point of view, the orb distorted Sidious's head and upper body. Sidious said, "I know you imagine a different life for yourself, Maul. An easier life than you have now."

Maul remained silent.

"I know you're upset about the snake that bit you," Sidious said, continuing around the watery orb until he had a clear view of Maul. "I know everything about you, Maul. Everything." Sidious edged around the orb until he was facing Maul again. "While you might think that your life is harsh and unpleasant, and that I am sometimes cruel, there is a reason for you to endure such pain. The reason is that you must become strong in every way. You must learn to overcome pain. Someday, you might become stronger than I. You'd like that, wouldn't you? To be stronger than I?"

"Yes, Master Sidious."

Sidious beamed at the boy. "Good." He glanced at the watery orb. "Ah! Look there, at those two fish."

Maul followed Sidious's gaze and saw a small fish with red and black stripes hovering beside a larger dark gray fish that had moved away from the other creatures to the bottom of the orb. Maul replied, "Yes, Master Sidious." He noticed that the smaller fish had yellow eyes, the same color as his own. The small fish stared back at Maul.

"How amusing," Sidious said. "If I didn't know better, I'd say those two were pretending to be *us*. If they were, I wonder where that would leave the rest."

Maul looked at the fish in the orb's upper area and saw them begin to jerk and spasm. Several fish puffed up twice their original size, shuddered violently, and suddenly deflated. Others rolled erratically through the water, their eyes bulging as their gills pumped furiously. But after a few seconds, all the fish except for the two at the bottom stopped swimming entirely and began drifting off in different directions. Some floated toward the top of the orb, but most sank down beside the two surviving fish, who continued to hover next to each other. As the fish sank, Sidious recited a strange verse.

> *"Far above, far above,*
> *We don't know where we'll fall.*
> *Far above, far above,*
> *What once was great is rendered small."*

Maul wondered what the words meant. He knew Sidious had somehow selected the two fish and maneuvered them to the bottom of the orb and caused all the others to die. He didn't know how Sidious had done this, but suspected it was some kind of magic. Looking away from the dead fish, Maul faced Sidious and said hesitantly, "Master Sidious . . . is it possible . . . to learn this power?"

Sidious smiled broadly, showing his teeth. "It is possible. But not immediately. You must be patient. I've prepared a training room. And today, you will receive personal instruction . . . from me."

Maul was surprised to hear about a training room and was instantly curious to see it. He hoped it was larger than the training area outside his own small room. As he wondered how soon his Master would show him the new training room, the six-legged droid, its two damaged legs replaced by a shiny new pair, sauntered back into the chamber.

Sidious glanced at the droid, then looked back at Maul and said, "Legs are not easily replaced. You do realize you must be punished, do you not?"

"Yes, Master Sidious."

"Always remember . . . a punishment is a lesson, young Maul. Learn it well. Now, come along." As Sidious stepped away from the floating orb, he waved his fingers at a tapestry that hung against one wall. The tapestry slid silently up toward the ceiling and revealed an open doorway built into the wall. Sidious walked to the doorway, which Maul assumed was a passage that led to the new training room.

Maul tried to step away from the orb, but his legs suddenly felt like they were heavy weights, anchored to the floor. He knew he would be punished even more severely if he did not obey his Master, but it seemed his own body—independent of his mind—was refusing to move. But before Sidious noticed Maul's hesitation, the droid reached out with a pincer and gave Maul a sharp jab in the back of his left thigh, causing him to jump forward. The droid muttered, "Don't make things worse."

As Maul began to follow Sidious, he glanced back at the bottom of the orb for a final look at the two surviving fish. The small yellow-eyed fish was hungrily biting into a dead fish. The large gray fish hovered a short distance away and appeared to be watching the yellow-eyed fish with some interest before its eyes shifted to look at Maul. Maul hurried into the passage, followed by the droid.

The training room exceeded all of Maul's expectations. So did his punishment.

But he survived.

CHAPTER TWO

The Brak iN

"Begin!" the droid said.

Maul ran fast across the training room floor, heading straight for the wall. Several months after his arrival in the training room, he was familiar with the routine. He launched off the floor with his left foot, hit the wall with his right, and ran several steps up the wall before he kicked away, flipping his body backward through the air. He landed on his feet, then sprinted back toward the wall and repeated the exercise again. And again.

And again and again.

The six-legged droid watched each move, making sure Maul performed the exercise exactly as Sidious had instructed. Sidious had told Maul that the exercise was designed to build strength, agility, and muscle memory. Sidious had also stressed that if Maul's timing was off and he flipped away from the wall incorrectly, he could wind up with a broken neck.

Maul continued the exercise until the droid told him to stop. As he landed on his feet, he felt his heart hammering within his small chest. He wanted desperately to rest on the floor, but resting was not allowed until the droid said so.

"Your timing has improved," the droid said. Rapidly extending one of its pincer arms, it swiped Maul with an electrode, giving the boy a shock.

Maul bared his teeth and snarled at the droid. Although he knew that the droid was simply carrying out Master Sidious's orders, teaching Maul to be prepared to deal with pain at any moment, he still resented getting shocks when he had not done anything wrong. The droid stared back at Maul through emotionless photoreceptors. Maul could anticipate many things, but he never knew when the droid was about to shock him. The droid was too fast.

However, Maul had learned much during his time with the droid in the training room. The room had special exercise equipment and weapons, as well as computer consoles that had been programmed to educate and challenge Maul's mind and mechanical abilities. He could identify hundreds of star systems, assemble complicated three-dimensional puzzles, and pinpoint the vulnerabilities of nearly every native creature on Mustafar. And in addition to running up walls, he could walk on his hands, climb swiftly up a rope, trot across a taut wire, and leap headfirst through an energy ring and come up standing.

"Go to console three," the droid commanded.

Maul went to the third computer console and seated himself before the computer's holoprojector. As he inserted both hands into the console's grip sockets, he wondered what the test would be about this time.

The holoprojector displayed a sequence of three different star systems and rotated each display so Maul could see the holographic stars and their respective orbiting planets from various angles. Then the computer cut off the projector, leaving Maul staring at empty air. The computer said, "Identify the second, first, and third systems, in that order."

"Malastare, Eriadu, and Denon," Maul answered quickly. He hoped the computer would next ask him to name the trade route that linked all three systems, because he knew the answer was the Hydian Way.

But the computer said, "The Malastare system includes three gas giants. Name the remaining planets that have more than one moon."

"Malastare and . . . Cogalle!" Maul said, his slight delay earning him a sharp sting in the palm of his left hand. Maul was still wincing in pain when the computer's audio speaker erupted with a recorded beast's roar.

"Identify the species," the computer droned.

"Tulrus." Maul suddenly felt searing pain in his right hand, and he corrected himself. "Northern tulrus!"

The questions continued for several minutes. Maul made only three more mistakes. When the computer was done, he removed his aching hands from the console sockets and massaged his knuckles. As he rose from his seat, the six-legged droid said, "Go to the ring."

The droid followed Maul to the ring, a circular platform that was elevated thirty centimeters above the training room floor. Maul hopped onto the platform while the droid ambled over to a nearby rack of weapons and selected a slender staff made of wood. Gripping the staff with a single pincer, the droid climbed onto the platform and faced Maul. "I will attempt to strike you. You will attempt to dodge the strike. Each successful strike or dodge counts as one point. Knocking an opponent off the platform counts as three points. The exercise ends when one of us has scored five points. Understood?"

"Yes." The word was barely out of Maul's mouth when the staff connected with the side of his left leg. He grunted in pain and anger.

"You forgot to jump," the droid said in a mocking tone. "My point."

The droid swung again, this time angling for Maul's right leg. Maul jumped. The droid let the staff's tip bounce off the platform and brought it up sharply to strike the bottom of Maul's right foot. Maul tumbled across the platform and came up standing, his eyes burning with fury at the droid.

"That must have hurt," the droid said. "The next strike will hurt more." The droid made a quick jab toward Maul, but the boy threw his body to the side and rolled, careful not to go over the edge of the platform.

"Your point," the droid said as it tossed the staff into the air. Maul ignored the airborne staff and kept his eyes on the droid. The droid caught the staff with a different pincer, then leaped forward. Maul dived under the droid, and as he somersaulted across the platform, he heard the staff whoosh past his head.

"Your point again," the droid said. "We are tied." The droid tossed the staff back and forth between three pincers, then seized it with a single pincer and rotated its arm so the staff spun like a propeller. The droid increased the speed of the rotation, transforming the staff into a barely visible blur.

Expecting the droid to advance toward him, Maul braced himself to jump away. He was not prepared when the droid threw the spinning staff directly at him, and he felt the slap of hard wood against the side of his face. The staff fell away from Maul and landed between him and the droid.

"I hope you are learning from this," the droid said. "The score is three to two." The droid stepped forward and reached for the staff.

Maul felt a rush of anger. The droid's pincer was still descending for the staff when the weapon leaped from the platform and flew toward Maul. Maul caught the staff with both hands as he glared at the droid.

The droid backed up. Maul held the staff out in front of him. He didn't know how the staff had sailed into his grip, and he wasn't sure what to do next. The droid had not mentioned that the staff could move by itself or said whether Maul would gain points if he obtained the staff or struck back at the droid.

"You've never done *that* before," the droid said, sounding surprised.

Maul didn't know what the droid was talking about. "The staff jumped. I . . . I only caught it."

"I must summon Master Sidious immediately." The droid's photoreceptors blinked and turned yellow as it transmitted a silent signal.

Maul wondered what he had done wrong. Then he wondered whether the droid might be trying to trick him by pretending to contact Sidious, and whether it might be preparing to attack again. The droid's photo-receptors flickered back to red, but it did not budge from its position on the opposite side of the ring. Maul continued clutching the wooden staff, his eyes locked on the droid.

Sidious entered the training room. Maul held tight to the staff but turned to his Master. Facing Maul, Sidious came to a stop at the edge of the elevated platform and said, "Tell me what happened."

"The droid and I were exercising, Master Sidious." Maul held the staff out before him. "This landed in the middle of the ring. Then it . . . it jumped up and landed in my hands."

Sidious nodded as if he understood. "Maul, what did you feel just before the staff jumped up?"

Maul glanced at the droid. "The score was three to two, Master. The droid was winning." He looked at Sidious. "I was thinking that the exercise isn't fair. The droid can hit me, but I can't hit back."

"Few things in life are fair, young one." Lowering his voice, Sidious continued, "But I did not ask you what you were *thinking*. I asked . . . what did you *feel*?"

Maul looked at the droid again. "I felt angry, Master."

Sidious smiled brightly. "Good. Good!" Without taking his eyes off Maul, he turned his head slightly and said to the droid, "Prepare my cruiser."

"Yes, Master Sidious," said the droid as it stepped down from the ring.

"Come along, Maul," Sidious said. "We're going for a ride."

Sidious's cruiser was a sleek vessel with a long prow, its aft area bracketed by angular fins that folded inward during landings. It raced through hyperspace, the dimension of faster-than-light travel. Sidious was on the cruiser's bridge and had left Maul alone, belted into the cruiser's passenger compartment. The boy sat quietly, his feet extending only a few centimeters over the edge of his seat.

Maul peeked through a rectangular viewport to see the luminous cascade of hyperspace. He had been excited to leave Mustafar, but he was also nervous, because he didn't know where his master was taking him or what the purpose of their journey was. Earlier, when they'd boarded the cruiser, Maul had briefly wondered if Sidious intended to take him to a faraway, extrasolar place to kill him. But after some thought, he decided it was unlikely that his Master would *take* him somewhere to kill him. If Sidious wanted him dead, he would not waste time traveling across hyperspace to get the job done.

The journey did not last long. Maul heard the cruiser's hyperdrive engine winding down. He continued gazing through the viewport. A moment later, the bright colors of hyperspace melted away and were replaced by a field of stars. The cruiser banked to port, and Maul saw they had arrived in the orbit of a small planet. He recognized a cluster of stars and realized they were still in the Atravis sector.

The cruiser descended to the planet's surface and landed. Sidious stepped into the passenger compartment, glanced at Maul, and motioned him to get out of his seat. As Maul unclasped his safety belt and lowered himself to the deck, Sidious passed his hand over a wall-mounted control switch, which simultaneously opened the starboard hatch and extended the boarding ramp. Maul followed his Master out of the cruiser.

"Welcome to Tosste," Sidious said.

A murky yellow sky hung over the bluish-gray terrain. Maul gazed across a wide area of mostly flat land and noticed some strangely angular rock formations in the distance. The ground was covered by sporadic clumps of stones and boulders. Maul saw no sign of movement.

"Take a good look," Sidious said. "We are standing upon what was once the bottom of an ocean. If it ever had a name, that name was lost to time many eons ago. Here, the only historic records are the geographic evidence." Sidious took a few steps away from Maul and looked toward the horizon. "It's hard to believe that Tosste was once home to billions of life-forms. While life on other worlds evolved and reached for the stars, Tosste's inhabitants were never so inspired. They stayed here. They died here. And what is their legacy? Nothing but fossils." He shook his head sadly. "To live without leaving a mark is a terrible thing. To die forgotten is even worse." He turned to face Maul. "It is . . . irresponsible."

Sidious's words chilled Maul. Was his Master implying that he was irresponsible? He wasn't sure. He stood very still and remained silent.

Sidious looked at the horizon again. "Walk with me."

Leaving the cruiser behind, they proceeded to a nearby outcropping of bedrock, which was bordered by a broad field covered by small stones. The tops of a few large boulders loomed over the stones. Sidious and Maul stopped at the edge of the bedrock. Surveying the stones, Sidious said, "What do you see?"

"I see rocks, Master Sidious."

Sidious frowned. Then he pointed to the center of the field of stones and said, "Go stand over there."

Maul always felt especially vulnerable when he could not see his Master, but he did as he was told, stepping across the stones until he reached the designated spot. He stopped.

"Turn around."

Maul turned to face his Master. Sidious stood with his legs apart, his hands clasped behind his back. Sidious said, "I suspect that every creature that ever lived on Tosste did not think much about rocks either. I had hoped that you would be smarter. I'll ask you again. What do you see, spread out on the ground all around you?"

Maul's yellow eyes darted back and forth. He saw only rocks. Some were pebbles, others large stones, and there were the tops of a few boulders. As ever, he did not want to disappoint his Master, but he did not know any other answer than the one he had already given. Returning his gaze to his Master's face, he said hesitantly, "I see rocks, Master Sidious. Thousands of rocks."

Something hard slammed into Maul's left shoulder blade. He ducked as he spun to confront his attacker, and as he moved, he saw the object that had struck him. It was a stone, which fell on the rocks near his feet.

Maul looked across the bluish-gray landscape. Not a trace of movement. No one had been standing behind him.

Another stone smashed into Maul's right bicep. He grunted as he spun again, this time to look back at his Master.

Sidious had not moved. His hands remained behind his back. But from the trace of a wicked smile on the Man's face, Maul suddenly knew the stones weren't flying by themselves.

Lifting his gaze to the sky, Sidious said, "The creatures that once roamed this now dead ocean, they lacked imagination. Ultimately, that is why they all perished. They failed to see . . . potential."

Potential?! Maul suddenly sensed a small stone whizzing toward his head. He raised his hand to deflect the stone as he ducked, but the stone sailed past his fingers and clipped one of his horns. "Weapons!" Maul shouted. "I see weapons!"

Sidious sighed. "The correct response is . . ."

"I see weapons, Master Sidious!"

"Not fast enough," Sidious said as a stone smashed into Maul's lower back.

Maul crouched and grabbed the nearest rock. He no sooner lifted it from the ground than he felt it burning into his hand. He yelped as he reflexively opened his fingers and let the rock fall. How could the rock have generated such intense heat? He suspected it was his Master's trickery.

"Oh, come now," Sidious said impatiently. "Almost any humanoid with fingers can do *that*."

Two stones smacked into the backs of Maul's legs, knocking him off his feet. He gasped as his small body fell on the hard rocks. Looking up, he saw two more stones rise from the ground. He twisted his body fast, trying to shield his head.

"Maybe I was wrong about you being special," Sidious said as he watched the two stones strike Maul. "Maybe you are just as useless and stupid as —"

Several stones hurtled up from the ground around Maul's body. Battered and bruised, Maul glared at Sidious. The stones sailed through the air, all heading straight for his Master.

Sidious whipped one hand out from behind his back and extended it before him. The rocks stopped in mid-flight, then fell to the ground. "Is that the best you can do?" Sidious sneered. "I should crush you now."

Maul snarled as he jumped to his feet and swiped at the air with both hands. Dozens of rocks launched up from around Maul and raced toward Sidious. Sidious moved his other hand out from behind his back and flexed his fingers. The approaching rocks rebounded as if they had struck an invisible shield.

Some of the rebounding rocks fell near Maul's feet.

Surprised, he stumbled back. He wasn't sure what had just happened.

"Well done, young one," Sidious said as the dust settled around him. "You passed the test." He began walking slowly toward Maul. "The droid told me that you moved the staff without touching it, but I had to see what you could do with my own eyes. Did you feel it? Did you feel the power of your anger?"

"Yes, Master Sidious," Maul responded automatically. Until that moment, he had not known that he had in fact been responsible for making the staff jump up from the ring in the training room. He looked at the rocks on the ground. He hadn't given any thought to launching them through the air either. He had just . . . done it.

Sidious came to a stop beside Maul. Looking down at the boy, he smiled and said, "I want to show you something. Stay close to my side."

Sidious extended his arms. Maul heard a rumbling sound and then saw stones sliding and bouncing away from two of the larger boulders that were about fifteen meters away, partially embedded in the ancient seabed. He realized the two boulders were rising slowly, as if an invisible giant were pulling them up from the ground. Dust and dirt fell away from both boulders as they tore free from the planet's surface. Maul watched with wonder as they ascended several meters into the air.

Sidious flicked his fingers. The two boulders launched even higher. He flexed his wrists, and the boulders spun around together like a pair of enormous dancers. He moved his hands apart, and the distance between the spinning boulders increased. Then Sidious clapped his hands together. Still spinning, the boulders swung into each other and collided with a thunderous crash. Shattered chunks and bits of rock exploded in all directions.

Watching the rocky debris rain down from the yellow sky, Maul said, "How, Master Sidious? How?"

"With the Force," Sidious said solemnly.

Maul looked at Sidious, hoping desperately to learn more.

"The Force is an energy field," Sidious continued. "It radiates throughout the galaxy. It is everywhere. It flows between all living things and every inanimate object. It is between us. It is between the stones, the cruiser over there . . ." He gestured to his starship. ". . . everywhere. Some beings — some very fortunate beings who are strong with the Force from the day they are born — are able to manipulate and control the Force. They can use its power to do incredible things. You and I, Maul, are such beings."

Maul looked at the two holes in the ground where the boulders had recently stood, then at the remains of the boulders strewn across the area. Knowing that such destructive power flowed through him made him feel very pleased. He smiled.

Seeing the boy's expression, Sidious said, "You and

I shall return to this world often. Here I will teach you the ways of the Force. But because the Force can be very dangerous to those who don't fully understand it, there is one rule you must obey. You must never reveal your powers to anyone else until I say you are ready. For now, the Force is our secret. No one else may know about it. Do you understand?"

"Yes, Master Sidious," Maul said, then quickly added, "But the droid saw the staff jump in the ring. Does the droid know . . . about the Force?"

"The droid knows just enough to help you in your training."

"Master Sidious, I meant . . . can the droid *use* the Force?"

Sidious chuckled. "No, boy. The droid is just a machine. Machines can't use the Force. But remember, the droid is a teaching tool. You are not allowed to use the Force against the droid."

"Yes, Master Sidious." Maul bit his lip.

"You have another question?"

"Master, you said I must not reveal my powers to anyone else. Who is 'anyone else'?"

Sidious pursed his lips, then said, "So far, you have lived a sheltered life, but it is only a matter of time before you encounter other beings. Most life-forms are oblivious to the Force. They don't realize that the Force binds the galaxy together. They cannot draw power from the Force." Sidious patted Maul's bruised shoulder. "Most people fear what they don't understand."

"Master Sidious, do you have to be angry to make the Force work?"

"Not all the time," Sidious said. "But it helps."

Maul stared at the ground. "Are there others like us, Master?"

Sidious knelt beside Maul so their eyes were on the same level. "Listen very carefully, boy. There are others who use the Force. But they are not . . . like . . . us."

CHAPTER THREE

The Jedi's esckap

"Tell me what you know about the Jedi, Maul."

Sidious and Maul were inside the training room in the Mustafar facility. Sidious stood beside the six-legged droid. The droid was operating a winch that controlled a long metal cable that extended to the ceiling. Maul was hanging upside down, his small body wrapped in chains, dangling from the winch's cable. Eight meters below Maul's inverted head was a large open vat of acid.

"I know only what I've learned from datatapes, Master," Maul gasped in response. Speaking was difficult because of the chain that was drawn tightly across his throat. His wrists were manacled behind his back, and as he struggled to free his hands, the droid began ticking at the winch's crank, slowly lowering Maul from the ceiling. He calculated that at the rate he was descending, he had about ten minutes to escape. "The Jedi," he continued, "are warriors who are strong with the Force. They use weapons called lightsabers. They are based on the planet Coruscant. They serve the Galactic Republic as peacekeepers."

Sidious smiled. "That's according to the data-tapes. But what I am about to tell you is the *truth*." He stepped away from the droid and began walking in a wide circle around the vat of acid. "The Jedi Order was founded twenty-five thousand years ago by a group of beings who were strong with the Force. Before the Jedi Order, such Force-sensitive beings were isolated instead of united. Some were regarded as wizards. Others as demons. There were not many. Nearly all were considered unique on their own worlds. They were strong, powerful individuals. Free to live and die as they wished.

"But the Jedi Order changed all that. They started by analyzing the Force to understand its power. They found it had a wide spectrum that was influenced by emotions. They debated their findings. Over time, they discovered there was much they could not under-stand, and they chose to believe what they wanted to believe. They believed some mysteries were best left unsolved. They believed that the Force itself was testing them. Like narrow-minded, superstitious children, they *created* explanations for the Force.

"And rather than embrace the full spectrum of the Force, the Jedi ignored the infinite shades of gray that stretched between light and darkness. They declared the light side of the Force was good and the dark was evil. To them, there could be no in-between, no middle ground." Sidious let out an exasperated sigh. "It's one thing to examine an energy field that permeates the galaxy. But to give an energy field characteristics of good and evil? One might as well say, 'That cloud wants to protect us from solar radiation, but that other cloud wants to strike us dead with lightning.'

"And then the Jedi declared that to be born with Force powers was not a gift or a curse. They insisted it was a *calling*. They proclaimed the Force should never be used for selfish purposes, that all Force-sensitive beings were obligated to use their powers for the benefit of others." Sidious shook his head ruefully. "Many Force users joined the Jedi Order, but the Jedi were not satisfied with their numbers. They sought out the so-called wizards and demons, and gave them three options. Join the Jedi, cease using Force powers, or die."

Sidious paused to look at Maul. Maul had traveled almost halfway to the acid vat. He had already wriggled his left hand out of the manacles and was now working to free his right.

"Join the Jedi," Sidious said. "Relinquish your individuality and freedom, and fight only when the Jedi tell you to fight. *Cease using Force powers.* One might as well tell an ordinary life-form to stop living. *Die. . . .* Well, I don't believe that requires an explanation. And

so, the Jedi not only increased their ranks but destroyed those who disagreed with them.

"The Jedi convinced the Galactic Republic that they could be the Republic's guardians. The Jedi Order thrived, and they expanded their authority beyond the Core Worlds. They used their powers and their lightsabers to vanquish those who opposed them. For many millennia, the Jedi were unchallenged. And they grew confident. So confident that they could hardly imagine the possibility that some Jedi did not *want* to be Jedi.

"But almost seven thousand years ago, a group of Jedi rebelled against their own kind. The battle that ensued lasted one hundred years. The so-called peacekeepers believed the war was over when they banished the surviving rebels to an uncharted region of the Outer Rim Territories. But the exiles did not meet their end in the Outer Rim. They discovered the Sith species, and they used their powers to conquer the Sith. They became the Sith Lords."

Sidious raised his right hand slowly and examined his fingernails. "Maul, in your studies of history and the galaxy, have you ever come across any datatapes about the Sith Lords?"

Maul had freed his other hand and was now bent at the waist, lifting his torso so he could work on the chains that were biting into his ankles. He glanced at Sidious and replied, "No, Master."

"That's because the Jedi destroyed many records."

Sidious flexed his fingers, then lowered his hand to his side. "The early Sith Lords had one ruler, the Dark Lord of the Sith, and their armies were legion. Eventually, they discovered the path back to Republic space and fought the Jedi in the Great Hyperspace War. They lost. But the Sith Lord Naga Sadow survived and managed to preserve his spirit in a tomb.

"Hundreds of years after Sadow's death, a Jedi named Freedon Nadd revived Sadow's spirit. Nadd became the new Dark Lord, and he used his powers to conquer the world Onderon. Following Sadow's example, Freedon Nadd also preserved his own spirit in a tomb. Many centuries later, Nadd's spirit was awakened by the Jedi Exar Kun, who became the next Dark Lord. Exar Kun allied with a wayward Jedi named Ulic Qel-Droma, and together they established a Sith Order ruled by two, a Master and apprentice. These two Dark Lords of the Sith failed to conquer the Jedi because they wound up fighting each other, as did their successors, another pair of former Jedi, named Revan and Malak. History, it seemed, was repeating itself." Sidious looked at Maul. "Am I going too fast for you?"

"No, Master." He was having some difficulty with the chains at his ankles, and he was close enough to the acid that the smell of it was burning his nostrils.

"I neglected to mention that Revan and Malak renamed themselves Darth Revan and Darth Malak. Some historians believe Darth is a contraction of *dark* and *Sith*, while others suggest it was a corruption of *daritha*, an ancient Rakatan word for 'emperor.' In any event, the honorific Darth was introduced to the Sith Lords. Following Revan and Malak, other former Jedi assumed the mantle of Dark Lords . . . and none learned from their predecessors' mistakes.

"History took a different turn about a thousand years ago, when yet another former Jedi, named Kaan, rose through the ranks of a new order of self-proclaimed Sith Lords. After Kaan became Dark Lord and united thousands of followers, he tried to avoid the mistakes of his predecessors. To avoid infighting, Kaan proposed that all Sith Lords were equals. Kaan's army became known as the Brotherhood of Darkness."

The droid's pincer lost its grip on the winch's crank. The metal cable slipped half a meter before the droid stopped the crank with another pincer. Maul's body fell and jerked violently in the air. He did not cry out but stayed focused on his shackles as he resumed his slow descent to the acid, which was now closer than he'd anticipated.

"At the Battle of Ruusan," Sidious continued, "the Jedi overwhelmed the Brotherhood of Darkness. With surrender not an option, Kaan crafted a Force-fueled weapon called a thought bomb, which would destroy all Force users within its blast radius. The thought bomb killed Kaan, his army, and many Jedi.

"But one Sith Lord survived. Darth Bane. Bane knew

that Kaan had been wrong to believe in strength in numbers. Bane knew that too many Sith Lords resulted in too much envy and competition. Everyone wanted to be the leader, the Dark Lord, and nearly everyone was willing to kill other members of the Brotherhood in order to achieve that goal. And so Bane established the Rule of Two. One Sith Master. One Sith apprentice." Sidious looked at Maul, who was still struggling with the chains, and added, "Any more would be to lose control."

Maul broke free, gripped the chain, and swung out, twisting his body in midair so he landed on his feet beside the acid-filled vat. He faced Sidious. Although he did not know his own age, he was now nearly as tall as Sidious's hip. He said, "Master, do the Sith Lords still exist?"

"I would not rule out the possibility," Sidious said. "Just remember, the Jedi do not tolerate Force users outside their order. It is because of them that you and I live in secret. Had they discovered you on Dathomir before I, they would have attempted to mold you into one of their own. A mindless, obedient servant for the Republic. Had they failed, they would have destroyed you. Now that you know the truth, how would you describe the Jedi?"

Maul thought for a moment, then said, "They are cowards, Master. Cowards and tyrants. They are weak."

Sidious smiled. "Do not underestimate the Jedi. Even though they have a fatal flaw, they are formidable."

"What is their fatal flaw, Master?"

"Compassion." Sidious looked at the chain that Maul had left swinging back and forth over the vat of acid. "You took much too long to free yourself. You will do the exercise again. But this time, the droid will lower the chain faster."

Maul bowed. "Yes, Master."

CHAPTER FOUR

The sith and Darth meal

"I have a surprise for you, Maul," Sidious said as he handed a cylindrical metal object to the boy. "Do you know what it is?"

"Yes, Master Sidious," Maul said as his eyes widened with awe. "It's a lightsaber. I've seen them on holovids."

They were on the planet Tosste, standing at the center of a grove of gnarled black trees at the edge of a desolate field, not far from Sidious's cruiser. Sidious had been bringing Maul to Tosste regularly over the past year, as the wide-open spaces allowed opportunities for training that could not be conducted on Mustafar's volcanic surface. Maul would run for great distances and perform long jumps. Under his Master's supervision, he fired ranged weapons and explosives and also practiced using the Force to lift and move objects. Maul never knew when Sidious would bring him to Tosste, or what plans Sidious might have for him there, but he always looked forward to any trip away from Mustafar.

Even if he was required to do rigorous exercises at their destination, he still regarded such excursions as adventures.

Maul turned the lightsaber over in his hand, testing its grip. He held it away from his body, just as he had seen Jedi hold their weapons in the educational holovids he'd studied in Mustafar's training room.

Sidious said, "What do you think?"

"It weighs less than I thought, Master."

"It's a training saber. The same kind used by Jedi younglings."

Maul wondered how his Master had obtained the weapon. But he didn't ask.

"That's the activation switch," Sidious said, pointing to a green switch on the lightsaber's grip. "Press it with your thumb."

Maul thumbed the switch. A brilliant amber blade of pure energy flashed out from the emitter at the end of the grip, accompanied by a loud hum. Holding tight to the grip with both hands, Maul could feel the power of the weapon. He grinned, unable to conceal his delight.

"That's it," Sidious said. "Feel the energy? Now, go on. . . ." Sidious made a waving gesture. "Test it."

Stepping away from Sidious, Maul made a tentative jab at the air, then swung the lightsaber back and forth. The weapon's hum changed pitch as the blade moved. Maul also noticed how the lightsaber illuminated the surrounding trees. He shifted his stance and faced a thick, twisted limb that jutted out from one of the gnarled trees. He looked to his Master.

"I know what you're thinking," Sidious said. "Will a training saber cut through that tree?" Sidious shrugged. "A Jedi would hesitate to share this information, but . . . well, I am not a Jedi. Training sabers *can* be adjusted for greater power, but the process is a bit time-consuming. You might try this instead." Sidious reached into a deep pocket, removed another lightsaber, and held it out to Maul.

Maul looked at the weapon in his Master's hand. He switched off the training saber, barely noticing how its humming sound fizzled out, and exchanged it for the proffered lightsaber. He noticed that the grip was heavier than the training saber's. He thumbed the activation switch.

A red beam flashed from the weapon's emitter and hummed to life. Maul immediately sensed that the blade was even more powerful. He looked again at the gnarled tree's limb, then glanced at Sidious. Sidious nodded. Maul jumped forward and sent the lightsaber's blade in a downward slash through the limb. He had expected at least to hear some kind of a cracking noise as the limb separated from the tree, but the blade sliced through the limb with a continuous whoosh, as effortlessly as a bird's wing slicing through air. And then the severed limb crashed loudly against the ground.

"Well done," Sidious said.

Maul swept the blade through the fallen limb again and again. With each sweep, he marveled at how cleanly the blade sliced through wood. From what he'd seen on the holovids, he knew the weapon was just as effective with dense rock and thick metal.

After he had reduced the tree's limb to diced chunks, he turned his attention to the tree's trunk and kept swinging. Sidious did not stop him.

When Maul finished with the tree, he reluctantly returned the lightsaber to his Master. Sidious said, "Now, it is time for you to meditate."

"Yes, Master." Maul turned and walked out of the grove, heading into the neighboring field. Sidious had trained him to relax his mind and body by closing his eyes and visualizing a dark, comfortable nothingness, leaving himself open to the power of the Force. Maul enjoyed meditating. It always left him feeling stronger.

He had taken only a few steps into the field when his foot struck something that moved. He looked down and saw a dinko.

From his studies, Maul knew about dinkos. They were nasty palm-sized creatures—not that anyone would want to pick one up. The dinko had powerful, perpetually moving rear legs that were naturally equipped with serrated spurs, two pairs of grasping claws on its chest, and extremely sharp fangs. The grasping claws were especially feared, as dinkos used them to grab on to a victim's finger or nose and would not let go unless surgically removed or killed. Even more notorious was the dinko's stinking venom. Because dinkos were native to Proxima Dibal, a planet situated on the far side of the galaxy, Maul wondered how a dinko had ever arrived on Tosste.

The dinko sprayed venom directly into Maul's face. Maul flinched as the venom hit him, stinging his eyes. He howled, then brought his boot down hard on the creature. He felt a certain satisfaction as he removed his heel from the crushed dinko and inspected its remains. Pleased at the way he had dealt with the dinko, he turned to look back at his Master.

"You flinched," Sidious said without pleasure. "You were afraid of the dinko?"

"Yes, Master. But I controlled my fear." Maul stated his claim with great certainty.

Sidious responded with a nod. But from experience, Maul knew his Master was displeased. He also knew a punishment would come.

They returned to Mustafar. Maul ate his evening meal as usual. He was not confined to a sensory-deprivation suit or forced to sleep on a hard floor. The atmosphere controls in his quarters were not turned off.

No punishment came the next day, or the next, or anytime soon. Eventually, Maul forgot about the dinko incident on Tosste.

And then one night, after a particularly exhausting series of exercises, Maul went to his quarters in the training room. After he entered his quarters, the door hissed closed behind him. He undressed in the darkness. Then he turned back the coverlet that was draped over his sleep mat, and a dinko jumped straight at him.

Maul was startled. He batted the dinko away but missed when he tried to stomp it to death. He hesitated, fearing that its claws would tear into his bare foot.

Another dinko jumped out from a corner. That dinko was followed by another, and then another. Maul realized the room was filled with the creatures.

The boy ran to the door and slapped the button to open it. The door remained shut. He tried to turn on the lights. The lights stayed off. In the darkness, one dinko jumped onto Maul's shoulder and dug its claws into his ear. Another latched on to one of his toes. Maul cried and screamed as he tried to shake them off. The dinkos sprayed their venom and blinded him. The stench was nauseating. Maul threw his body against the walls in a desperate attempt to crush them.

It took Maul almost an hour to kill all the dinkos. When he was done, he passed out on the floor of his gore-filled quarters.

The door did not open until the next morning. It slid back to reveal Sidious standing in the doorway. He looked at Maul's inflamed skin, swollen eyes, and bloody hands and feet. He said, "Do not flinch again."

Maul understood. He learned. He obeyed. And after his test against the dinkos, he never ever flinched.

CHAPTER FIVE

"Hold still," said the six-legged droid as it wiped blood from Maul's rib cage.

Maul squirmed on the edge of the metal table and said through clenched teeth, "You have the bone-knitter on the wrong setting."

"No, I don't," said the droid as it moved the medical tool deeper into the wound on Maul's left side. Then it repeated, "Hold still."

They were in the expansive training room in the Mustafar facility. Five months had passed since Sidious had begun training Maul in lightsaber combat. In recent days, the droid had been teaching him how to throw blades with great accuracy, and also how to dodge and catch blades that the droid threw at him while he did his exercises. As for running up walls and flipping backward to the floor, Maul had become so adept that he could do it with his eyes closed. However, he had been unprepared when, a few minutes earlier, he had kicked away from the wall and straight into one of the droid's waiting pincers.

The droid set aside the bone-knitter, then sprayed an exotic salve over Maul's skin. "You should be relieved that Master Sidious was not present when you allowed me to break two of your ribs," the droid said. "He would have been most displeased."

"I didn't *allow* you to break my ribs," Maul said as the droid began wrapping a bandage around his torso. "I thought you were standing near me to watch me exercise."

"Well, you know what Master Sidious would say." Adjusting the pitch and tone on its vocabulator to perfectly mimic Sidious, the droid rasped, *"To leave yourself vulnerable is an open invitation to death."* Switching back to its usual voice, the droid said, "Still, I'm sorry. I didn't mean to hurt you. It was an accident."

The droid's words surprised Maul. The droid had never before imitated Sidious or apologized to Maul. No one had ever apologized to Maul before. Maul said, "I will be more careful next time." Then he looked at the droid's red photoreceptors and added, "Do you have a name? I learned from the computer that many droids have names."

The droid responded with a chittering noise that sounded like a cross between grinding gears and laughter. "I was programmed and engineered for training and discipline. My designation is TD-D9. If you wish, you may call me Deenine."

"Thank you, Master Deenine."

The droid chattered again. "No. Just Deenine."

"Oh." Maul was suddenly curious about the droid. "Have you always been on Mustafar, Deenine?"

"No, I've visited other worlds. I've been to Coruscant, Naboo, and . . ." The droid flicked its photoreceptors to face Maul and said, "Forget I said that. You didn't hear that from me."

"I won't tell."

"Good. You may put on a shirt now."

Maul eased himself off the table and reached for the shirt he'd been wearing earlier. It now had a hole in it, where the droid's pincer had torn through the fabric, and was stained with blood. But before Maul could pick up the shirt, the droid snatched it and added, "You may put on a *clean* shirt."

Maul walked across the training room and stepped through a doorway to enter his quarters. Nearly twice the size of his former room, his quarters had a lighting system that he could control, a sleep mat with a coverlet, and a small trunk for storing clothes. It also had a door that he could open from inside or outside. Except when Sidious or the droid locked him up, he was generally free to go to the training room at any time.

But there was one thing his quarters lacked. A window.

Maul's former room had been in almost every way unmemorable, but it had had a view. He had spent many

54

hours scanning the rocks for Mustafarians and their lava flea mounts, but his memories of that time seemed increasingly dim. Back then he had wished for a view of a different world. Now he wondered if he would ever see the lava flowing into the fiery sea again.

He reached into his trunk and removed a clean black shirt. He thought it was strangely kind of the droid to suggest that he should wear a clean shirt. He had learned about friendship from an educational recording, which showed how some creatures lived and worked together without harming each other. He wondered if the droid might be his friend.

Maul pulled the shirt on and felt a stab of pain at his left side. He gnashed his teeth and took a series of quick and shallow breaths through his nose, careful not to expand his lungs so much that they'd make his ribs hurt. He wondered how long it would take for his ribs to heal.

As he exited his quarters, he said, "Deenine, when will my ribs—?" He stopped short when he saw Sidious standing beside the droid. He had not heard Sidious enter the training room.

Sidious was holding Maul's torn, bloodied shirt. Sidious looked from the droid to Maul and said, "Maul, tell me what happened."

Maul glanced at the droid, then said, "I was training, Master Sidious. I ran up the wall, and when I jumped away from it, Deenine stuck out a pincer and broke two of my ribs. It was an accident. Deenine didn't mean to hurt me."

"Really?" Sidious said. "I didn't know the droid was capable of doing anything accidentally. Or that you and . . . 'Deenine' were on familiar terms." Still holding the torn shirt, Sidious faced the droid. "Is it true? Did you injure Maul by accident?"

"No, Master Sidious," the droid said. "When Maul leaped from the wall, I raised my pincer knowing that it would break his ribs if he did not adjust his body in midair."

"So why did Maul think it was an accident?"

"Because I told him it was an accident, Master Sidious."

"In other words, you lied?"

"Yes, Master Sidious. I lied."

Sidious looked back at Maul. "Have you learned anything from this, Maul?"

Maul glared at the droid. He felt betrayed and angry. He could not believe he had trusted the droid. Looking back at Sidious, he said, "Yes, Master Sidious. I have learned I must not trust anyone. I must be ready to attack and fight back at all times."

"Excellent," Sidious said as he tossed the torn shirt onto the metal table. "And because 'at all times' includes right now, you will now repeat the exercise you were doing with the droid. Only this time, you will avoid breaking any more ribs." Sidious gestured to the nearest wall. "Begin at once."

The droid made a chittering noise, then said, "I beg your pardon, Master Sidious, but I suggest you allow Maul's ribs to heal before he attempts to —"

"I do not recall asking for anyone's opinion," Sidious said, keeping his eyes on Maul. "Especially an opinion from someone who is an admitted liar."

The droid offered no response.

"Now, Maul," Sidious continued, "what *you* said is absolutely true. You *must* be ready to attack and fight back at all times. If your bones were broken during a fight with an actual enemy, do you think that enemy would wait for you to heal before attacking you again?"

"No, Master Sidious."

Sidious gestured again at the wall. "The droid will stand near while you run up the wall and leap back to the floor. At any given moment, the droid might attack. And the droid will not hold back because you are already injured. Do you understand?"

"Yes, Master Sidious."

Glancing at the droid, Sidious added, "Do you understand?"

"Yes, Master Sidious." The droid shuffled over to the wall and waited for Maul to run.

Maul went straight for the wall. He tried to ignore his broken ribs, but with each step, he felt the sharp pain intensify. He did not cry out. He would give neither his Master nor the droid the satisfaction of hearing him cry. He was angry at both of them, especially at the droid. He let the pain feed his anger, let his anger feed his strength. He ran up the wall several steps before he kicked off, keeping his left arm close to his side to prevent the droid from striking his rib cage again.

Maul did not think the droid would attack on his first flip away from the wall. He was still in midair when the droid lashed out with violent force. Maul felt his left arm snap as the droid's swat knocked him clear across the room. Maul crashed into the opposite wall and then everything went dark.

When Maul opened his eyes, he was lying on the sleep mat in his quarters. His upper left arm was heavily bandaged. He pushed himself up carefully. Every part of his body hurt. Moving his right hand over to his left side, he felt that the bandages were wet with blood. And then he noticed a familiar shadow fall across the floor from the doorway.

"Master Sidious is very displeased," said TD-D9 as it stepped into Maul's quarters. "Very displeased with both of us."

Maul noticed the droid was carrying a medkit. He looked away from the droid and faced the wall. "Go away and leave me alone."

"Your bandages need to be changed."

"I said go away!"

"But if don't apply bacta, your wounds won't heal. They'll become infected and—"

"You keep your claws off me! I'll take care of myself!"

The droid chattered a mechanical sigh, then placed the medkit on the floor beside Maul's sleep mat. But as the droid retreated for the doorway, it paused and said, "There's something I want to tell you, Maul. I want you to know that I—"

"I don't care what you have to say," Maul interrupted. "You're a liar."

"That's right, I lied," TD-D9 said. "But I didn't lie to you. I lied to Master Sidious."

Maul listened.

"When I told Master Sidious that I lied to you, that was a lie. The truth is that I accidentally broke your ribs. But if I had told Master Sidious the truth, he would have destroyed me."

Maul looked away from the wall and scowled at the droid. "Are you also going to tell me that breaking my arm was an 'accident' too?"

"No, Maul. I did that on purpose. It was the only way to immediately end the exercise. I did not want to prolong your pain. I did not want to hurt you. I hit you so hard that I knocked you out because I did not want Master Sidious to hurt you more than that."

"You broke my arm!"

"I'm sorry for that. But I believe Master Sidious would have done worse."

Maul thought about this, then said, "What makes you think I won't tell Master Sidious that you lied to him?"

"If you do, he'll replace me with another droid. Maybe he'll replace me with a droid who actually enjoys inflicting pain." The droid sighed again. "I told you I'm sorry. Your bandages really do need to be changed."

"I'll do it myself," Maul said sullenly. "I don't want to talk with you anymore."

The droid walked out through the doorway, leaving the medkit behind. Maul looked at the medkit and wondered if his Master or the droid had done something to the bandages so he would be in even more pain after he put them on.

He faced the wall that was opposite the doorway. He thought of the tapestries that decorated the walls in Sidious's chamber, and how one tapestry concealed the passage to the training room. He wondered if a secret passage might be hidden behind the wall right in front of him.

Too weak to walk, he crawled over to the wall and pressed his right hand against it. The wall did not yield to his pressure, but as he removed his hand from its surface, he saw he had left traces of blood. He had forgotten that he had touched his wounded side earlier.

He recalled his Master's words on Tosste: *To live*

without leaving a mark is a terrible thing. To die forgotten is even worse.

Maul reached to his wound again, then extended his index finger and drew a vertical smear of blood directly onto the wall. He then drew another vertical line to the right of the first one and then added two horizontal lines that connected with the vertical lines to form a rectangle. Next Maul concentrated on the area within the rectangle. It took him just over twenty minutes to fill the rectangle with a drawing of what he remembered of Mustafar from his view through the window of his old room. By the time he was done, he felt very tired.

Maul crawled back onto his sleep mat and lay down again, positioning his head so he could look at the drawing he'd made with his own blood. He wished he could leap into the drawing and run away. He was still looking at the drawing as he drifted off to sleep.

When Maul next awoke, he was still in his quarters but dressed in fresh bandages. He realized that TD-D9 must have taken care of him while he was sleeping. He also noticed that all the walls had been cleaned, and that his drawing had been completely erased.

TD-D9 appeared in the doorway. Maul frowned at the droid. TD-D9 said, "Master Sidious instructed me to bring you to him now."

Maul decided it was best to not mention the drawing. He thought it would hurt for him to get up, but he felt surprisingly better than he had earlier. He suspected the droid had given him medicine while he had slept. Leaving his quarters, he followed the droid out through the training room and up through the passage that led to Sidious's private chamber. As they walked, Maul said, "Deenine, do you know if Master Sidious intends to kill me?"

"I don't think so," TD-D9 replied. "He has invested so much time into your training that I suspect he wants you to stay alive. But I don't think you should have drawn that picture on the wall."

Maul's steps did not falter as he continued following the droid, but his mind was suddenly racing. He wondered what consequence he might suffer because of the drawing. He said, "Did Master Sidious see the drawing?"

"I don't know. I erased it right after you fell asleep."

"Then how would he even know about the drawing . . . unless you told him?"

"I didn't have to tell him," TD-D9 said. "You should know by now, child . . . Sidious knows everything."

Before Maul could ask the droid any more questions, they exited the passage. They found Sidious standing beside the hovering watery orb. Maul noticed that the orb had been restocked with living fish. He spotted the two survivors of the previous menagerie lurking at the bottom of the orb. The big gray fish was looking away from Maul, but the smaller one with red and black stripes had one yellow eye fixed on the boy.

The striped fish had grown larger since the last time Maul had seen him.

Sidious looked at Maul, then frowned. "Tell me, do you think I've been rough on you?"

"No, Master Sidious."

"You do understand that your training serves a greater purpose?"

"Yes, Master Sidious."

Sidious smiled. "I suspect that others might question my teaching methods, but I am glad you do not. I can assure you that you are an excellent pupil. Not once did you cry out during your recent exercises. Not once. You are an exceptionally strong boy, and you are becoming stronger every day."

"Thank you, Master Sidious," Maul said as he bowed, ignoring the pain of his aching ribs.

Sidious raised his eyebrows. "Now, there is another matter that has come to my attention. Evidently, you are not entirely satisfied with your quarters. You miss the view that you once had of Mustafar. Is this correct?"

Without hesitation, Maul replied, "I was not thinking clearly when I drew a picture on my wall, Master Sidious."

"You have no wish to return to your former room?"

"No, Master."

Sidious smiled again. "I didn't think you would want to go back to that little box. But if you missed the sight of Mustafar, you should have told me. After all, seeing

Mustafar is something that can be easily arranged." Sidious waved a finger at TD-D9.

The droid responded by firing a tranquilizer dart into Maul's neck. Maul collapsed to the floor. TD-D9 did not attempt to break his fall.

A loud roar awakened Maul. He coughed as he inhaled hot, acrid fumes, and his eyes stung as he opened them. He saw darkness overhead, and for a moment, he thought he was in a cave. But then he noticed the darkness was moving and alive with dancing bright red stars. And he suddenly knew what he was really looking at.

Dark clouds. And drifting, burning ashes.

He pushed himself up. He was on a broad slab of rock on Mustafar's surface. The loud roaring sound came from a nearby rocky vent that was spewing lava. He didn't know how long he'd been outside or even how far he was from Sidious's facility. But he knew he had not arrived at this place on his own.

He looked around. He saw no sign of TD-D9 or Sidious, or of any kind of shelter. Although they had not taken away the clothes and bandages he was wearing, they had not left him with any provisions. But he did have something to his advantage. He had his training.

Maul was not scared. He felt free. He could live or perish on this hostile world without anyone to tell him what to do. And then he realized he was not in any way eager to die. He became resolved to survive. He would do anything and everything necessary to stay alive.

He saw a dark shape move past the lava vent. Crouching low to the ground, ignoring the pain from his ribs and left arm, he watched with wonder as a tall, masked Mustafarian rode by on a massive six-legged lava flea. Two more flea-mounted Mustafarians followed.

Maul had no idea where the Mustafarians were headed, whether they were going to a mining camp or back to their remote village. He would track them, find their food, and steal it. If it became necessary to kill them to ensure his own survival, he would gather rocks to strike them dead or strangle them with his own bandages and broken bones. And then he would find his way back to Sidious and prove that he was indeed a strong boy. He would prove that he feared nothing.

He would earn the respect of his Master.

The three Mustafarians moved off. Maul followed them.

CHAPTER SIX

the reven

"Ah, you have returned," Sidious said to Maul, who stood before him in the tapestry-decorated chamber in the Mustafar facility. Sidious was holding a small container of food pellets, which he had been gently pushing into the hovering watery orb to feed the fish. Maul's head was covered with soot and dirt, and his torso was adorned with ill-fitting, bloodstained Mustafarian armor. Looking at the armor, Sidious smiled. "I see you kept busy during your little outing."

The spider-legged droid TD-D9 stood a short distance behind Maul. The droid's right front leg was missing, and one of its left legs was mangled. "I found him outside, Master Sidious," TD-D9 said, "not far from the landing pad. He'd set a trap. I walked right into it." Raising one of its pincer arms, the droid held out the shattered remains of its front right leg. "Maul could have destroyed me."

Sidious set aside the fish food and looked at Maul

skeptically. "Is this true? You could have destroyed the droid?"

"Yes, Master Sidious," Maul replied.

"Then why didn't you?"

Maul tilted his chin toward the droid. "Because I wanted to bring this thing back to you in pieces."

Sidious smiled again. "Maul, do you know how long you were running around on Mustafar's surface?"

Maul grimaced. "I'm not certain, Master Sidious. I fell asleep twice while I was outside."

"Well, I'll tell you, then. You survived outside for seventeen standard days. I doubt very much that many boys your age—and that includes young Mustafarians—could accomplish such a thing without a wealth of provisions and emergency equipment. I commend you."

Maul bowed, holding his left arm away from his side as he did so.

Sidious noticed the angle of Maul's arm. "You didn't heal properly. Your arm must be broken again and reset. Is it painful?"

"Yes, Master Sidious," Maul said flatly, his tone not even slightly betraying his extreme discomfort. Out of the corner of his eye, he spied the red and black striped fish with yellow eyes swimming near the larger gray fish at the bottom of the nearby orb that was suspended above the circular dining table. The yellow-eyed fish appeared to have grown bigger again.

Sidious looked to TD-D9 and said, "Take Maul to the training room. Attend to his arm. Clean him up. And then bring him back to me."

"Yes, Master Sidious," the droid said, then added, "Afterward, do you wish for me to repair my own legs?"

"Yes, of course," Sidious said.

Leaving Sidious, TD-D9 hobbled after Maul to the training room. Neither spoke once, not even while the droid reset Maul's broken arm. Thirty minutes later, they returned to Sidious's chamber. Maul was wearing fresh clothes. His left arm was wrapped in a bacta splint.

Sidious was seated at the dining table beneath the watery orb. Fine cutlery, dinner plates, and drinking goblets were on the table. Facing TD-D9, Sidious said, "You may repair yourself after you bring us dinner."

"Yes, Master Sidious," said the droid, hobbling out of the chamber again.

Sidious looked at Maul as he gestured for the youth to sit in the chair across from his own. Maul was surprised. His Master had never before invited him to dine in the chamber. And because he was extremely hungry, he also felt grateful. Maul bowed to his Master before he sat down. The fish swimming in the watery orb overhead made shimmering shadows across the table's surface.

"This is a momentous occasion," Sidious said solemnly as he dragged his finger around the rim of his goblet. "Because my presence is increasingly required on other worlds, I have arranged for you to attend the Academy on the planet Orsis. It is an institution for training paramilitaries for planetary governments. They also train intelligence agents, mercenaries, and assassins, as well as supplying professional combatants for the gladiatorial arenas. It's a very exclusive school. To be an Orsis cadet is considered quite an honor."

Maul was astonished. The prospect of leaving Mustafar and attending a school with other students was almost overwhelming.

"The director of the Academy," Sidious continued, "is a Falleen named Trezza. He's a bit short and almost two hundred years old, but do not let that fool you. He is as tough as they come, and mind tricks will not work on him. But there are a few minor challenges. Trezza does not know my name and he never will. And to protect my identity, I shall wear a disguise. Understood?"

"Yes, Master," Maul said, although he could only imagine why his Master wanted to protect his identity.

"You may use your own name, but there is one catch, and this is very important. You are not allowed to use your Force powers on Orsis unless you are alone with me, and unless I grant you permission. When time allows, I will continue to train you in the ways of the Force while you are on Orsis, but you must never use your powers against any other students or faculty members under any circumstances. You must never even talk about your powers to anyone else on Orsis. If you disobey this command, the consequences will be most dire. Understood?"

"Yes, Master." He knew what *dire* meant.

Sidious poured a dull-colored liquid into the goblet set before Maul and then his own. Raising his goblet to Maul, Sidious said, "To future endeavors."

As Sidious and Maul drank, TD-D9 hobbled back into the chamber carrying a tray that held plates covered by domed lids. The droid set the covered plates before the seated figures, then said, "Are you finished with me, Master Sidious?"

"Most definitely," Sidious said. Keeping his eyes on Maul, Sidious waved at the droid. TD-D9 lifted off the floor, flew across the chamber, and smashed into the wall. The impact was so great that Maul noticed small shock waves ripple across the suspended orb. The droid's photoreceptors went dead as its ruined body collapsed in a loud crash.

Maul didn't flinch. He thought of all the time he'd shared with the droid, how it had reared him and punished him, and how he'd never expected his Master to destroy it. He wouldn't have the chance to say goodbye, or to destroy the droid himself. All these thoughts raced through his mind, but he didn't flinch.

Smoke began rising from the droid's shattered head. Sidious grinned. "Not the most efficient way to eliminate an old droid we don't need anymore, but that *did* feel good. Now, let's see what's for dinner." Ignoring the smoldering droid across the chamber, Sidious lifted the lid off his plate and revealed there was nothing on it. He sighed. "Oh, well, I wasn't very hungry anyway. How about you, Maul? What's on your plate?"

Maul had no idea what kind of game his Master was playing. He hoped he would find food on his plate but braced himself for disappointment. He removed the lid from his plate to reveal the red and black striped fish he'd watched grow over the past four years. Lying on its side, the fish stared back at him through one eye. Maul saw the fish's gills flex and realized it was still alive.

Maul didn't flinch.

The fish's eye shifted to look at its former home, the orb above the table, where other fish continued to swim. Maul doubted that Sidious expected him to pick up the fish and insert it back into the orb.

"Go on," Sidious said. "Dig in."

Maul obeyed. He tore into the fish, starting with the head. As he ate, Sidious said, "We will leave for Orsis tonight. Do you have any questions?"

"Yes, Master," Maul said between mouthfuls. "What will be your disguise on Orsis?"

"Naturally," Sidious said, "I shall present myself as a man with a lack of vision."

CHAPTER SEVEN

"Welcome to Orsis Academy," hissed the short male Falléen, a reptilian humanoid with green skin, as he stepped away from the massive desk in his office to greet the two people, a man and a boy, who had just entered. "I am Trezza, the Academy's director."

"Thank you for receiving us," said the man, who wore a bulky old set of cybernetic goggles, a sensor-laden metal bracket that completely concealed his eyes and most of his forehead. He clutched a walking stick in one hand and had his other hand placed on the shoulder of his young companion, who wore loose-fitting black clothes. "Allow me to introduce you to Maul."

Trezza had already noted the boy's horns and tattooed visage, and assumed he was a Zabrak. Trezza bowed slightly and said, "Greetings, Maul. You may call me Master Trezza."

Maul bowed deeply. "I am honored, Master Trezza."

Returning his attention to the sensor-goggled man, Trezza said, "And how shall I address you, sir?"

Sidious sighed. "With all due respect, I prefer to remain nameless. For practical purposes."

"Very well," Trezza replied with a smooth smile, making it evident that he was no stranger to clients who valued privacy above all else. "So, you came here to discuss . . . ?"

Sidious smiled. "As I mentioned in the holomessage that I sent, I am a modest businessman. But I anticipate my business will expand greatly in years to come and that competition will increase. I shall require a very dedicated bodyguard. One with a good set of eyes. You may have noticed I am somewhat ocularly challenged." Sidious lifted his walking stick and tapped its handle twice against the side of his sensor goggles. "Maul's vision is exceptionally good, and his loyalty is beyond question."

Trezza glanced at Maul again, then returned his attention to the goggled man. "Do you have a certain time frame for when you expect Maul to be . . . sufficiently *grown* for such a job?"

Sidious chuckled. "My mind is quite made up about Maul. I can afford to wait. I trust you have received the credits I sent for his registration and tuition?"

"Yes," Trezza hissed. He picked up a datapad and examined a readout. "Your payment is in order. However, Maul does have to take a standard physical examination.

Also, his age was not indicated on the registration. Our administration would like to know that and some other data for placement purposes and general record keeping."

"For confidentiality reasons," Sidious said smoothly, "I would prefer not to divulge Maul's age. I also request that he not be prodded by any medical droids unless he receives injuries that require immediate attention. I have already made a contribution in addition to the other fees, but I am quite willing to pay more to ensure . . . privacy."

"That won't be necessary," Trezza said. "Your contribution was exceedingly generous, and very much appreciated. If it is your wish that we keep no records of the boy's enrollment, I personally guarantee that there shall be no records. However, there is one thing we must address. Even though we're a long way from Coruscant, the Jedi Order forbids Orsis Academy from training Force users."

Neither Sidious nor Maul flinched. Sidious smiled and replied, "You are most perceptive, Master Trezza."

Trezza tapped the side of his nose. "My nose and I have been around a long time, and we've met all types. I can smell Force users. I suspect you're aware of the Jedi Order's rules and regulations, that they expect me to report any Force-sensitive applicants, but here's another fact for you. I really don't care much for the Jedi. The way I see things, if a cadet is Force-sensitive, that's the cadet's business. Just don't make it *my* business." He looked at Maul. "I don't know what kind of powers you have, son, but while you're on my property, no use of the Force. If you can't handle that, you will be expelled. Am I clear?"

Maul bowed. "Yes, Master Trezza."

"You are most accommodating," Sidious said with a polite nod.

"We shall take excellent care of Maul."

Sidious grimaced. "I wouldn't want you to show him any favoritism."

"Of course not," Trezza said. "I meant only that he will receive the very best education in the arts of combat." Trezza redirected his gaze to Maul. "Would you like to have a look around the school?"

"Yes, Master Trezza."

Sidious smiled as he patted Maul's shoulder. "I believe I'll join you." As they exited Trezza's office, Sidious moved his walking stick back and forth, tapping at the floor in front of him.

Orsis Academy was a sprawling compound. Bordered by a tall wall that was topped by security sensors and automated weapons placements, the school consisted of nine interconnected buildings, three large open courts, and an open field beside a starship landing pad. Sidious's cruiser rested on the pad next to a drop ship that had just arrived from the aptly named Orsis Orbital Station, the large space station that traveled in a geosynchronous orbit with the planet. In broad daylight, the station was visible as a point of light in a fixed position in the sky.

As Trezza guided Maul and Sidious to a wide walkway that spanned two buildings, Maul spotted a stairway that led down to a beach along the seashore. He felt a pang of excitement as he took in the view. He was still having a hard time believing that his Master had brought him to Orsis, that his years of isolation on Mustafar might actually be behind him.

Maul glanced at his Master. Sidious had explained that the sensor goggles were a necessary disguise because he did not want to be recognized on Orsis. Maul wondered, *Why would anyone here recognize Master Sidious?*

Trezza led Maul and Sidious across the walkway, which overlooked one of the open courts. Trezza said, "We place as much importance on computer skills as we do on poison production and assassination techniques. And Orsis offers many opportunities for training programs beyond the walls of the Academy. As cadets mature and progress, they learn to fight and survive in the mountains, forests, deserts, and seas. We have hunting grounds and . . ."

A loud clattering sounded from the court below. Sidious stopped short with Maul and said, "What's that racket?"

"Some of our younger cadets are exercising with combat staffs," Trezza explained. "If you step closer to the rail, you can see them . . ." Remembering his guest's sensor goggles, he added, "Oh, please forgive me."

"That's quite all right," Sidious said, his mouth twitching into his smile as he reached up to adjust his goggles. "I can usually see shapes well enough, just not much detail."

Trezza motioned for Maul to guide Sidious closer to the railing. Maul looked down and saw several dozen cadets, mostly humanoid adolescents, swinging wooden combat staffs at each other. Thanks to his studies on Mustafar, he could identify each cadet's species. A pair of bug-eyed Rodian boys seemed to be the noisiest with their weapons. Both Rodians were testing their staffs against a Nautolan girl, an amphibian with tentaclelike tresses extending from her head. The Nautolan moved quickly and appeared to be very capable of defending herself.

"Right now," Trezza said, "we have just over five hundred cadets. As you know, we offer programs for ages eight years old and up. Most have enrolled for four- or eight-year programs. We also have a good number of 'floaters,' temporary students who come here to refine their skills. Graduates also come back from time to time for the same reason."

Sidious said, "Bounty hunters?"

"Occasionally. Do you object?"

"Not at all. On the contrary, I've met a few very accomplished bounty hunters in my time." Sidious stroked his chin thoughtfully. "I've heard your instructors include a Mandalorian who once fought Jedi. I believe his name was Krakko. Meltch Krakko. Is it true he's the best?"

Trezza stared quizzically at Sidious's goggles, then looked back at the cadets below. "He's still *among* the best, but I regret to inform you that your information is dated. Commander Krakko left us some time ago, returned to his clan. As you may be aware, the Mandalorians are engaged in a civil war."

"Oh, now that *is* unfortunate," Sidious said as he patted Maul's shoulder. "I really had hoped the boy might receive training from a Mandalorian. You see, Maul has been in a few fights, but . . . well, he can be a bit wild. He lacks finesse. He needs to learn how to make each move count. I don't suppose you have another Mandalorian about?"

Maul was surprised and embarrassed by his Master's description of him, but he kept his expression neutral. He almost missed the irritation in Trezza's voice as the Falleen replied, "Commander Krakko was our *only* Mandalorian instructor. But I'm confident that we can still teach young Maul here some things that he can't learn anywhere else." Trezza looked at Maul. "I've already agreed to forgo the standard physical examination for you, Maul. But now that I'm aware you've 'been in a few fights,' I would appreciate a demonstration of your abilities."

Maul looked to Sidious. Sidious adjusted his goggles and said, "A demonstration? I suppose that does sound like a practical way for you to evaluate Maul."

Trezza led Maul and Sidious into a lift tube and they descended to the court. As Maul stepped out onto the same level as the cadets, he suddenly realized they were all taller than he. Every one of them.

Seeing Trezza, the cadets halted their exercises, lowered their combat staffs, and bowed to him. Trezza gestured to Maul and said, "We have a new cadet. His name is Maul. I'm told he can fight."

One of the Rodians laughed out loud. Trezza shot him an icy look. The Rodian shut his snout.

Trezza cleared his throat. "I'm looking for a volunteer. Will any one of you fight the new cadet?"

Maul did not expect every cadet to raise an arm, tentacle, or equivalent limb into the air and shout in unison with the others, "I volunteer, Master Trezza!"

Trezza looked at Maul. "Remember what I said about the rules on my property, son."

"Yes, Master Trezza." Maul looked at Sidious.

Sidious adjusted his goggles, leaned close to Maul, and whispered, "Select the largest and most muscular student. Introduce yourself. Hurt him. No killing."

As Maul's gaze traveled across the cadets, he peeled off his black shirt, exposing his lean, tattooed torso. He was aware of the many eyes gazing at the bold red and black patterns on his bare flesh. He placed his shirt neatly on the ground. Stepping away from Sidious and Trezza, he overheard one cadet whisper, "Check out his ribs."

Maul breezed past the malodorous Rodians and came to a stop before a teenage Abyssin, a hulking native of the planet Byss. Distinguished by a broad head that held a single eye with a slit pupil over a broad, fleshy nose and a mouth full of sharp teeth, the Abyssin stood nearly two meters tall. Maul tilted his head back, looked up into the Abyssin's eye, and said, "I am Maul. Your move."

The Abyssin's nose twitched, and then he blinked his eye in disbelief. When he had volunteered to fight the boy less than a minute earlier, he had never imagined the boy would actually choose him. His eye flicked to see Trezza. Trezza nodded to him.

The Abyssin shifted his feet. Maul stood his ground. All the other cadets stepped back, leaving room for the combatants.

The Abyssin launched a sweeping kick that knocked Maul off his feet, and then lashed out with one hard-muscled arm that connected with Maul in midair. Maul flew across the courtyard and crashed to the ground. Both Rodians roared with laughter. Trezza did not reprimand them.

The Abyssin leaped forward, landing on his powerful legs a short distance from his opponent, and waited for Maul to rise. Maul shook his head as if he were making sure nothing was loose as he slowly pushed himself up from the ground. Once he was on his feet, he turned to face the Abyssin again. Maul threw a jab at the Abyssin's left thigh, just above his knee.

If the Abyssin felt the jab, he didn't show it. He pivoted on one foot and kicked out with the other, catching Maul in the stomach. The sound of the impact made a few cadets wince. Maul was again lifted off his feet. Hitting the ground, his body rolled like a broken doll past several cadets until he came to a stop near the feet of the female Nautolan. The Nautolan looked down at Maul's small, tattooed back, then turned to face Trezza and said, "With all due respect, Master Trezza, this is *not* a fair fight."

"What's that?" Sidious said as he tapped his walking stick against the ground. "Did Maul do something unfair?"

"Not at all," Trezza said. "He simply chose to go up against an older cadet."

"He does have spirit," Sidious said. Then he muttered, "Curse these old goggles. I can't see a thing."

Maul braced one palm against the ground. His arm trembled as he pushed himself up. The Abyssin stepped closer to Maul, moving up behind him. Maul started to turn to face the Abyssin, but then his legs buckled and he collapsed. Maul squeezed his eyes shut, then opened them. He looked at a cloud overhead, then shifted his gaze to see the Abyssin. Maul gasped, "What's . . . your name?"

The Abyssin blinked at the boy for a few seconds but finally replied, "Dalok."

Maul twisted his neck away from the Abyssin and his horns dug into the ground. His chest shuddered and then his limbs went slack. He turned his head again, and his eyes rolled up into their sockets before they shifted back to stare in the general direction of the Abyssin. "Your name," Maul repeated. "Please . . . tell me . . . what's your name?"

The other cadets quietly moved in around the Abyssin to get a closer look at the defeated boy. Seeing that Maul was thoroughly beaten, the Abyssin knelt beside him, leaned over his face, and said, "I just told you. My name's Dalok. Are you all ri —"

Maul grabbed the back of Dalok's head, pulled Dalok's face up against his own, and sank his teeth into Dalok's fleshy nose. The startled Abyssin screamed. With his teeth and one arm, Maul held tight to Dalok's head while he moved his other hand to grab Dalok's throat.

The surrounding cadets recoiled. Dalok tried to roll away from Maul, but Maul stayed on him, slamming and driving his knees into the nerve clusters in the Abyssin's shoulders. Dalok was flat on his back as he convulsed, his arms flopping uselessly beside him. Dalok passed out.

Maul rose to stand beside Dalok's unconscious body. Turning slowly, he looked at every one of the surrounding cadets, letting them see the Abyssin's blood dripping down his chin and notice that he wasn't even breathing hard. He thought he smelled fear from the female Nautolan who had tried to call off the fight. He didn't know how old she was, but noted she was slightly taller than he. When his yellow-eyed gaze fell on the Rodians who'd laughed at him, he spat at the ground.

An astonished Trezza looked at the goggled man beside him. "You said Maul has been in a few fights. Just how many is 'a few'?"

"I'm not sure, really," Sidious said with a shrug. "Obviously, I never actually *saw* any of his fights. Tell me, did he win this one?"

"He almost beat his opponent to death."

"Did he, now?" Sidious chuckled as he elbowed Trezza. "I *told* you he was a bit wild."

The Nautolan moved past Maul, and one of her head tresses brushed against his arm. She knelt beside Dalok and checked his pulse. Looking to another cadet, who stood gaping nearby, she said, "His nose will heal but he needs a medpac." As the cadet went for the medpac, the Nautolan turned to face Maul. Maul could see his own reflection in the Nautolan's large black eyes. Although he could not comprehend why, he did not want her to be afraid of him.

Keeping her eyes fixed on Maul, the Nautolan said, "You *did* know that Dalok's an Abyssin, didn't you?

That Abyssins have regenerative abilities?"

In fact, Maul was already aware of this, but that particular bit of knowledge had not crossed his mind when he'd challenged the Abyssin. He'd simply selected the largest and most muscular student, just as Sidious had instructed. Maul looked away from the Nautolan and let his gaze flick back and forth at the Rodians' snouts. "No," he lied. "I didn't know."

The Rodians trembled. Maul knew he was going to enjoy his time at Orsis Academy.

CHAPTER EIGHT

"I want to go swimming," said the female Nautolan, whose name was Kilindi Matako.

Maul did not know why Kilindi was talking to him. He had been at Orsis Academy for almost three years, and the other cadets always kept their distance from him during his recreation hours. He continued dragging his vibroblade along the edge of the long branch he was carving into a spear. But when Kilindi didn't walk away, he realized she might be expecting a response, so he said, "Then you should go swimming."

They were in the open courtyard closest to the sea at Orsis Academy, near a gateway to a path that led down to a rocky beach. On the far side of the courtyard, a group of cadets was preparing for the upcoming martial arts competition against a rival military school.

"I thought you might want to come with me," Kilindi said.

Surprised, Maul cast a sidelong glance at her and said, "Why?"

"I don't know. I just thought you might. I thought maybe you liked to swim."

Maul's jaw tensed as his memory flashed back to Mygeeto, a planet of ice and snow in the Outer Rim Territories. During a break from the Academy, Master Sidious had brought him to Mygeeto to exercise and test his Force powers. They had been walking by a lake that was covered by a sheet of dark ice. Even though Maul had worn heavy, insulated clothes, the frigid winds cut like lasers against his skin. He had just completed a series of exercises that had him running up sheer, icy slopes and then coming down as fast as he could. He knew he had performed well, and he'd hoped that his Master might praise him.

Instead, his Master raised a hand and used the Force to lift Maul's small body, tossing him into the middle of the lake.

Maul crashed through the ice and sank, his heavy clothes and boots pulling him down. As the freezing water bit into his face and chilled his blood, he feared he would die. And then his Master's words came to him. . . . *Turn your fear into anger.*

It was easy for Maul to be angry, especially with his Master. The dark side ignited and fueled his anger. He was enraged by the icy water and by the entire planet Mygeeto. He fought his way to the surface, kicking and clawing and bursting through the ice. And after he broke through the ice, while he was still gulping freezing water and struggling to keep his face above the surface, he saw his Master on the shore.

His Master made no move to help him.

Maul's rage was incredible. His fury propelled his arms and legs, made him push through the water, kick his booted feet, and swim to shore. The dark side had set an inner fire to keep him alive, but he quickly realized that same fire did little to keep him warm. He was shivering fiercely as he arrived before his Master.

And even then, his Master did not praise him, but merely continued their walk by the lake, with Maul staggering along at his side, hating the cold, hating the water, hating everything. . . .

"Well," Kilindi said, "I guess I'll see you later." She turned away from Maul and began walking toward the courtyard's gate.

"Wait," Maul said. He switched off his vibroblade and set it down beside the spear he'd been working on. He said, "I like to swim."

Maul marveled at the way Kilindi moved through the sea, her long head tresses trailing behind her. He thought she was even more graceful in the water than she was on land. Not that he would ever tell her.

He was standing in the sea, not far from the shore, just up to his waist, his bare arms held out stiffly at his sides. Kilindi was swimming about thirty meters beyond him, her strong legs cutting through the water without any obvious effort. He watched her submerge and was surprised when just a few seconds later she broke the surface a meter away from him.

Gazing at Maul with her large, dark eyes, Kilindi said, "Is something wrong?"

"No," Maul said.

"But you said you liked to swim, and you're just standing there."

Maul grimaced. "It's been a long time. Since I've been in water."

"Oh." Kilindi glanced at the shore. "Do you want to go back?"

"No." Maul moved his hands back and forth in the water. "I . . . I like being here."

Kilindi lowered her body so just her head and shoulders were above water. "I like it here too. There weren't any seas like this where I grew up."

"I don't understand," Maul said. "You are a Nautolan. Your homeworld is Glee Anselm. An ocean planet."

"But I didn't grow up there," Kilindi said flatly. "You knew that, right?"

Maul shook his head. Because he had not grown up on Iridonia or Dathomir, he felt foolish for having assumed Kilindi came from her people's homeworld.

"I thought it was common knowledge," Kilindi said. "I've heard other cadets talking about it, so you were bound to find out. Before I came to the Academy, I was on Orvax Four. I was a slave."

Although slavery was outlawed on Republic worlds, Maul knew that it existed throughout the galaxy. His mind was suddenly filled with many questions about Kilindi's past, but he said nothing, because he had no reason. He didn't need his Master to tell him that the girl's life should not be of any interest to him. And yet he was interested.

"But all that's behind me now," Kilindi continued as she tilted her head back and looked up at the sky. "My owners are dead."

Without thinking, Maul blurted out, "You killed them?"

Kilindi lowered her head so she faced Maul again. "Yes. They were a large family. I killed them all."

Maul thought, *Good.*

"Killing them was easy, but leaving Orvax was hard. Lots of slavers were hunting me. But Master Trezza heard about the killings and . . . well, he found me before anyone else did. He's the reason I'm at the Academy. I'm his ward. You knew *that*, right?"

"I knew you were Master Trezza's ward," Maul said. "That's all."

"So now you know about me. What about you? Where are you from?"

Maul looked down and watched the water ripple at his fingertips. "I can't say."

Kilindi tilted her head curiously. "Because you can't say, or because you won't?"

"Both," Maul said, then shook his head. "We can't talk about . . . me."

Kilindi shrugged, the movement making her head tresses jiggle. "Never mind. I won't ever ask personal questions again. But I do have some advice for you."

Feeling suddenly irritated, Maul said, "Why should I want *your* advice?"

"Because I know why you're making your own wooden spear."

That got Maul's attention. "I'm listening."

"Master Trezza invited you to go hunting wild kaabores with him and told you it's a tradition at Orsis Academy for cadets to make their own wooden spears for their first kaabore hunt. But it's really a test to see if you're prepared for the unexpected. I'm guessing he'll lead you straight to a pack of armored chargrecks. That's what he did to me on my first hunt. See these scars?" Rising so her upper body was above the water's surface, Kilindi turned to show Maul the three jagged marks across the back of her left shoulder. "A chargreck did that. Your wooden spear will be useless."

Maul eyed Kilindi suspiciously. "Would Master Trezza be very angry with you for telling me this?"

Kilindi nodded. "Very."

"Then why? Why tell me?"

Kilindi grinned. "Because I'm hoping you will tell me about the look on Master Trezza's face when you pass his test." And then Kilindi sent her body backward, sliding into the water and launching away from Maul. She took care not to splash him as she left.

Maul lowered his body into the water up to his neck, then held his breath and kept his eyes open as he dropped below the surface. He could clearly see Kilindi, illuminated by shafts of sunlight as she undulated past a school of fish. He still hated the waters of Mygeeto, but he decided the sea of Orsis was not entirely unpleasant.

He thought about what Kilindi had told him. He had been looking forward to his hunting expedition with Trezza, but now, even more so.

Four days later, Maul was with Trezza in an outback to the north of Orsis Academy when Trezza pointed to the ground and whispered, "Look there. Kaabore tracks, and they're fresh. I'm guessing there's one just beyond those trees."

Maul shifted his long spear in his hands as he looked toward the trees. Keeping his voice low, he said, "Shall I try flushing it out, Master Trezza?"

Trezza smiled. "Be my guest."

Holding his spear with one hand, Maul moved past the trees, down a short hill, and around some tall shrubby growths before he saw the five armored chargrecks that were waiting for him, just as Kilindi had anticipated.

Each chargreck's body was protected by incredibly strong segmented plates lined with sharp spikes.

Maul reached to his belt with his free hand and grabbed a small packet. All the chargrecks hissed and lunged at him at the same time. He threw the packet at them as he flipped backward. He was still arcing through the air as the packet exploded open with a quiet pop and deployed a wide electroshock net. The chargrecks hit the net and were instantly stunned. They thudded to the ground a split second before Maul landed on his feet.

Maul glanced behind him. No sign of Trezza. He set his spear aside and moved fast. He deactivated the net, which he had taken from the Academy's munitions room, then bunched it into a tight ball and stuffed it between the branches of one shrubby growth. He gathered his spear, then walked back up the hill and past the trees before he found Trezza. Trezza said, "Find anything?"

"No kaabore, Master Trezza," Maul said casually. "Just a few chargrecks."

Trezza's reptilian gaze bore into Maul's eyes. "Chargrecks? Out here? Are you sure?"

"I think so, Master Trezza. That is, they *looked* like chargrecks."

"What happened? Did they run away?"

"Oh, no, Master Trezza." Maul shifted his spear from one hand to the other. "I killed them. I just didn't think anything of it because I was looking for a kaabore."

Trezza glanced at Maul's spear and then back at the boy's face to see if he was lying. Trezza said, "You killed them? With that spear?"

"No, Master Trezza. I killed them with my hands."

Trezza's nose twitched, and he looked very confused as he said, "You didn't use the Force. I'd have smelled it on you."

"I know you would have, Master Trezza."

Maul could hardly wait to tell Kilindi about how he had used the electroshock net, and also about Trezza's reaction. But he wouldn't tell her what Trezza had said about the Force. He always kept in mind his Master's warning, that no one other than Trezza could know about his powers, because if anyone found out . . .

The consequences will be most dire.

CHAPTER NINE

a Attack

Crouched behind the wide trunk of an ancient tree, Kilindi Matako stayed in the tree's shadow as she surveyed the steep, rocky cliff at the edge of the forest. She glanced at Maul, who was hunkered down beside her, and whispered, "Ready?"

Maul nodded. Six years had passed since his arrival on Orsis. Taller and stronger, he still did not know his own age, but based on his observations of similar humanoids, he assumed he was about thirteen years old. Although he was already considered a master of numerous martial arts, he still had difficulty working as part of a team.

Except when he was partnered with Kilindi.

Kilindi moved first, diving away from the tree so she rolled across dead leaves and came to a stop behind another trunk. A sudden burst of blaster fire tore at the ground between the two trees. A second burst pounded into the opposite side of the tree that Kilindi had moved behind. The trajectory of the blaster bolts indicated the shots came from the top of the cliff, about six meters above Kilindi's position. She glanced back to where she'd left Maul, but he had already vanished. She waited.

Barely ten seconds later, Kilindi heard a horrific scream from atop the cliff. A blaster fired, and then another voice wailed across the forest. When the screaming stopped, a third voice called out, "Mission accomplished. All clear." The third voice was Maul's.

Kilindi moved around the tree and walked out into the open, heading for the base of the cliff. It took her almost a full minute to scale the wall of rock. As she climbed, she sighted three spherical remotes hovering out of the forest and rising into the air. She knew that the remotes belonged to Master Trezza, and that he used them to track cadets during exercises.

When Kilindi reached the top of the cliff, she found Maul standing a short distance from two fellow cadets, the Rodians Hubnutz and Fretch. The Rodians were clutching at their respective right arms, sitting on the ground beside the shattered pieces of their blaster rifles.

"Thanks a lot, Maul," Hubnutz snorted sarcastically. "Nice of you to only fracture our arms this time."

A repulsorlift engine sounded from overhead, and Kilindi and the Rodians looked up to see Master Trezza's shuttle approaching from Orsis Academy. The three remotes glided up to the shuttle and secured themselves to a rack on the vessel's sensor array.

"Oh, isn't that terrific?" Fretch said. "Now we get to listen to Trezza lecture us on how we messed up."

"Yeah, Maul, you're a real prince," Hubnutz said as the shuttle landed.

Maul ignored the Rodians and the shuttle as he stood at the edge of the cliff, gazing over and beyond the forest canopy, staring in the direction of the distant mountain range that was broken by Blackguard's Gorge, where Sidious had acquired an old fortress to be used as his private retreat during visits to Orsis. With Trezza's permission, Maul was allowed to travel by speeder bike to the fortress, where his Master continued to train him in the ways of the Force and also lightsaber combat.

My Master is there now. Waiting for me.

Fretch saw Trezza climb out of the shuttle, then angled his snout at Kilindi and added, "Hope you had fun showing off for your pet slave."

"I'm not a slave!" Kilindi said, her head tresses whipping off her shoulders as she whirled to face Fretch. "And I'm no one's pet!"

"Good one, Fretch," Hubnutz said. "You hit a nerve in Maul's slave." The two Rodians laughed wheezily.

Maul kept staring at the mountains on the horizon.

Kilindi scowled. It was common knowledge that she had served as a slave before she arrived at Orsis Academy. If she had any inclination to respond to the laughing Rodians, she refrained when she saw Trezza walking toward them. Hubnutz and Fretch rose to their feet, grunting from the pain of their injured arms. Kilindi noticed that Maul had not budged, that he was still gazing over the forest. She whispered, "Master Trezza's here."

Maul turned and directed his gaze to Trezza, who was carrying a datapad. Trezza came to a stop beside the Rodians, and the four cadets bowed to him. Trezza bowed his head slightly, then said, "Hubnutz and Fretch. You failed to defend the cliff."

"Maul busted our arms again," Hubnutz whined.

Trezza frowned with disappointment at the Rodians. "If you can't defend yourselves against an opponent you already know, how do you ever expect to deal with the unknown? You must be—"

"But Maul's not like other people!" Fretch protested.

Trezza's green brow furrowed. "You interrupt me again, young Fretch, and you'll find yourself in solitary confinement for a week."

Fretch bowed. "Forgive me, Master Trezza."

"As I've told you too many times before, you must be more mindful. You must learn to think like your enemy, to anticipate every measure with a countermeasure. If you are not prepared for the unknown, the unknown will strike you dead."

"Yes, Master Trezza," the Rodians said in unison.

Turning to Maul and Kilindi, Trezza said, "You are to be commended for your stealth. I confess, I could not keep track of you two. My remotes lost sight of you after you evaded the third patrol in the canyon, before you reached the forest. I know that canyon well. Did you stray into a cave?"

"Yes, Master Trezza," Kilindi answered.

"Why?"

Kilindi glanced at Maul. Maul said, "Because the remotes were revealing our position to our opponents. Before the exercise, I overheard Hubnutz and Fretch talking. They placed trackers on your remotes."

"You couldn't have overheard us," Fretch said. "Hubnutz and I were alone in the barracks when we talked." And then Fretch noticed Trezza glaring at him.

Hubnutz said, "It was Fretch's idea!"

Trezza sneered at the Rodians. "I'll deal with you two later." Returning his attention to Maul and Kilindi, he said, "Come with me. We have a very special appointment." Trezza began walking back to his shuttle.

Special appointment? Maul's expression remained passive, but his mind raced as he wondered what Trezza wanted with him and Kilindi. He started walking with Kilindi, following Trezza, and was halfway to the shuttle when he said, "I forgot something." He went back to the Rodians.

Seeing Maul approach, Fretch said, "Thanks for squealing on us."

"Yeah," Hubnutz said. "You're a real pal."

"Don't make things worse," Maul said. "Trezza wants to see us shake hands."

"Why?"

"He didn't say."

As Fretch carefully extended the hand at the end of his fractured arm, he glanced at the shuttle and said, "But Trezza's not even looking at us."

Maul grabbed three of Fretch's long green fingers and twisted them sharply. The noise of rapidly snapping bones made Fretch gasp and Hubnutz cringe. Fretch made a sick gurgling noise.

"Either of you ever call Kilindi a slave again," Maul said, "I'll tear your arms off and feed them to you."

Maul released Fretch's broken fingers and headed back for Trezza's shuttle. He boarded the shuttle and took a seat in the passenger compartment across from Kilindi and Trezza. Trezza was consulting a timetable on his datapad, oblivious to what Maul had just done to Fretch. After the shuttle lifted off, Maul was not at all surprised to see they were headed for Blackguard's Gorge.

Trezza looked up from his datapad and said, "Kilindi, have you met Maul's Master before?"

99

"No, Master Trezza. But I have seen him on occasion, when he's visited the Academy. May I ask . . . are we going to his retreat?"

"Indeed, we are." Trezza looked at Maul and said, "I remain astonished that your Master managed to obtain Blackguard's Castle. The previous owner made it clear to everyone in the Orsis system that he had no intention to sell."

If Trezza had asked Maul how his Master had obtained the castle, Maul would have respectfully and truthfully answered that he did not know. Because Trezza's comment had not been a question, Maul remained silent. He knew Kilindi was also wondering why they were traveling to meet with his Master. He glanced at Kilindi, who was peering through a viewport to see the land below.

Snaking between the treacherous cliffs of two snow-capped mountains, Blackguard's Gorge was a long valley that had been named, according to legend, after an ancient space pirate who had used the gorge as his hideout for decades. The only structure in the gorge was Blackguard's Castle, a modest fortress that hugged the shadowy vertical slab of a steep cliff. The castle was essentially invisible to the naked eye, because its rough exterior blended in perfectly with the colors and textures of the mountain. Even the landing pad, at a glance, resembled nothing more than a wide shelf of broken rock.

Trezza's shuttle touched down on the landing pad, and a tall, wide rock made a rumbling sound as it traveled on ancient mechanisms, sliding back from the mountain wall to reveal a concealed hangar. Exiting the shuttle, Kilindi was the first to spot Maul's Master. He was standing in the spacious hangar's entrance, holding a walking stick in one hand and wearing the sensor bracket that concealed the upper half of his face.

"Greetings," Sidious said to the group. "Please, come with me. Our guest is waiting inside." He tapped his walking stick across the landing pad, motioning the others to follow him.

Guest? Maul was intrigued. Except for him and occasionally Trezza, Maul was unaware of anyone ever visiting his Master at the castle.

Sidious's cruiser was parked on the far side of the hangar, which also housed a technical station, assorted tools and supplies, and a few empty cargo containers. The walls were solid rock. Sidious grinned impishly as he led Trezza, Kilindi, and Maul to the center of the hangar. Maul had a strange feeling inside the hangar, a feeling he couldn't quite define. *Almost like . . . we're being watched.*

"You didn't tell them about our guest, did you?" Sidious said to Trezza.

"No," Trezza said, shifting his datapad so he held it behind his back. He looked at Maul and Kilindi. "Recently, the Orsis Academy faculty and I realized we had a problem. A problem concerning you two."

Maul sensed Kilindi was alarmed by Trezza's announcement. He found it hard to understand why she couldn't at least pretend to remain calm.

"Perhaps I should rephrase that," Trezza continued. "The problem was not with you, but with our existing faculty. There was little more that the instructors could teach either of you about stealth tactics or hand-to-hand combat techniques, and yet you have two more years ahead of you at the Academy. In short, you require greater challenges than the other cadets. Now, I mentioned this problem to a certain businessman." Trezza gestured to Maul's Master, who smiled sheepishly. "Maul, your Master suggested a former instructor who only recently became available again. Your Master also made a generous donation to enable Orsis Academy to secure this instructor. And now, it is my honor to introduce both of you to—"

Sidious cleared his throat loudly. Reaching up to adjust his sensor bracket, he said, "Excuse me, Master Trezza, but I'm very curious about something. I wonder how Maul and Kilindi will react if they meet their new instructor *without* knowing any more details in advance."

"But of course," Trezza said. "Why don't you and I move over beside your cruiser and give these young people some room? May I guide you?"

Sidious tapped his walking stick against the floor

and said, "That's very kind of you, but I *do* know my way around here."

Leaving Maul and Kilindi at the center of the hangar, Sidious and Trezza went to the cruiser and turned to face the cadets. Sidious leaned close to Trezza and said, "Let me know when anything interesting happens."

Kilindi said, "I have a bad feeling about this." And then she gasped and grabbed the back of her neck, her knees buckling. Maul caught her around the waist and pulled her against his body as he launched sideways, carrying her with him. In midair, his right hand swept up Kilindi's back until his fingers touched a small dart in her left shoulder blade. He hit the floor with the girl on top of him, absorbing the impact as he plucked the dart out from her shoulder. He rolled away from her and was still clutching the dart as he rose to stand, gazing in the direction of the dart's trajectory.

He saw a figure, a man who wore dark gray body armor and whose head was concealed by a helmet with a distinctive T-visor. The armored man held a dart pistol in one hand and had a missile launcher secured to his back.

A Mandalorian.

Maul knew about Mandalorians, whose warrior heritage dated back thousands of years. He also knew that two factions of Mandalorians had battled each other in a long civil war, and that the war had ended recently. And he recalled that his own Master, after their arrival on Orsis six years earlier, had talked with Trezza about

103

a former Academy instructor, a Mandalorian who had once fought Jedi.

Maul was fast enough to see the Mandalorian's incredibly swift approach. He was also fast enough to dodge the first kick that came at his head. But he wasn't fast enough to stop Meltch Krakko's fist from knocking him out cold.

CHAPTER TEN

they Look

Running fast along the volcanic mountain slope on Orsis, Maul gnashed his teeth as another low-energy blaster bolt tore through the thin fabric of his utility suit and slammed into his back. He ignored the pain and kept running.

His pursuers were Meltch Krakko and the two Rodian cadets, Hubnutz and Fretch, and the goal of their exercise was to capture Maul. Krakko and the Rodians were wearing mimetic suits, energy-powered cloaks that allowed for almost perfect camouflage in any environment. Since Krakko's return to Orsis Academy two years ago, he had not only taken a special interest in training the Rodians in tracking and sharpshooting, but also in tormenting the fifteen-year-old Zabrak.

For Maul, the current exercise was merely a warm-up for a bigger challenge on Orsis, an Academy rite of passage called the Gora. Named after the challenge's location, an immense volcanic crater filled with dense forests, vast swamps, and bloodthirsty beasts, the Gora required a cadet to traverse the crater for seven days, surviving without food or equipment except for a single vibroblade. From what Maul had heard, being chased by camouflaged hunters was nothing compared to surviving the Gora.

Maul approached the rim of the mountain's valley, where glacial water and wind had carved a maze of tall, rocky formations. He darted into the labyrinth, never pausing to catch his breath. More blaster bolts zinged past his body. If his pursuers' blasters had been set to kill, he would have been dead already, a fact that infuriated him. But because Sidious and Trezza had forbidden him from revealing his Force powers to Orsis faculty and cadets, he was obliged to let his pursuers shoot him occasionally. If he'd dodged *every* blaster bolt, they would have had ample reason to suspect he was a Force user.

Without glancing back, he drew his own blaster, which was also set at nonlethal power, and returned fire. He felt his rage increase as he deliberately missed his attackers. Although their mimetic suits rendered Krakko and the Rodians practically invisible, Maul had no difficulty sensing their exact positions behind him. He could have shot each one of them with his eyes closed, but that would have been against the rules that Sidious and Trezza had established. And so he pretended to miss Krakko and the Rodians, let them believe he was an ordinary Zabrak, and sometimes allowed himself to be hit.

A blaster bolt slammed into his calf, and another into his right shoulder. The pain did not slow Maul but he pretended to stumble anyway, all in his ongoing effort to conceal his powers. But as he ran forward, he saw he was heading straight for a deep chasm. Although he was confident that his incredible strength and agility would have enabled him to leap to the other side of the chasm, he knew it would be a mistake to make such a jump with Krakko and the Rodians watching. However, he was also determined to evade his pursuers, to show them that he was more daring than they could ever imagine.

I'll earn their respect.

Maul kept running right up to the chasm's upper ledge, then flung his body into the gap, aiming not for the opposite ledge but for the wall below it. He used the Force to cushion his impact against the wall, then extended his arms to hook his hands over an outcropping a few meters below the ledge. With his legs dangling in the air below him, he made every movement look desperate, even though he was not in the least afraid.

He sensed movement above, and knew Krakko and the Rodians were searching for a narrower gap so they could follow him across the chasm. They succeeded less than a minute later, and Maul looked up to see them leaning out over the ledge. He assumed the exercise was over, that they would lower a rope to bring him up.

A rock struck his horned head, and another hit his shoulder. He heard a scuffing noise from above and realized his pursuers were kicking rocks over the rim. As a rock struck the back of one hand that clung to the overhang, he knew he hadn't earned their respect at all.

They're trying to kill me.

Maul was done with restraining his powers, and pretending to be something that he wasn't. Summoning the Force, he launched himself from the overhang and sailed up and out of the chasm. He somersaulted and twisted in midair, flipping his body over the three camouflaged hunters so that he landed on his feet, facing their backs. Startled, Krakko and the Rodians turned fast. Maul had already drawn his blaster and opened fire at them at point-blank range.

Krakko grunted and the Rodians cried out in pain as the blaster bolts hit them. They jumped and rolled away from the chasm's edge, firing back at Maul. For a moment, they moved as if their mimetic suits still gave them an advantage over their prey. Maul used the Force to avoid being hit while he rapidly squeezed and released his blaster's trigger, moving his arm back and forth to aim and fire at each of his cringing targets. He didn't miss once.

Hubnutz and Fretch tried to find protective cover. Maul shot at their legs and continued shooting them after they fell and began screaming. Krakko deactivated his own mimetic suit so he was fully visible. Facing Maul, he shouted, "Stand down!"

Maul fired at Krakko.

"Stand down!"

Maul pretended he didn't hear Krakko over the blaster's report. He felt the blaster start to overheat but kept firing.

And then an amplified voice from above bellowed, *"Cease fire!"*

Maul lowered his blaster as he looked up. He saw an airspeeder approaching. Trezza was behind the airspeeder's controls. The Falleen's expression was outraged.

Maul knew Master Sidious would be even less pleased.

"You're not entirely to blame for what happened," Sidious said, his face lost in shadow beneath his dark blue cloak.

Maul stood before his Master on the stone floor in the cavernous main hall of the fortress at Blackguard's Gorge. After Trezza had treated Maul's wounds and informed him that his Master had already arrived on Orsis to observe the exercises, he had traveled by speeder bike from the academy to the fortress. Because he had been repeatedly told not to reveal his powers, he knew his punishment would be terrible.

"The dark side has taken a serious interest in you," Sidious continued. "And is gauging if you might be a proper vessel for its power. Seeking expression and loathing restraint, the dark side tests us continually, competing with our will and our need for secrecy."

"Yes, Master," Maul said. "I was overcome."

"Overcome?" Sidious's eyes blazed beneath his cowl. Maul looked down at the stone-cold floor.

"I said that you weren't *entirely* to blame," Sidious said bitterly. "The willingness of the dark side to cooperate in your pitiful demonstration doesn't exonerate you from breaking your vow to me and from jeopardizing my plans."

Maul had not wanted to disappoint his Master. He wanted to apologize and ask for forgiveness, but he knew if he did, his punishment would be even worse. And then he thought of how long he had suffered on Orsis because he had not been allowed to use his powers, and he felt his shame transform into rage. He looked up at Sidious and was about to speak but his Master made a pinching gesture. Maul felt his throat constrict.

Sidious walked a few steps away from Maul before he released his remote grip on Maul's throat. Looking back at Maul, he continued, "You have called unwanted attention to yourself. The Jedi have been continuing to harass Trezza for creating assassins and proxy armies, so consider what might have happened had a Jedi been present during the exercise. A Jedi would not only have grasped that you are strong in the Force, but that you have received training in the dark arts, endangering *my* position."

Maul felt crushed. He thought of all his years of training, his constant effort to please his Master. He reflected on the exercise that had ended at the chasm, tried to imagine escaping his tormentors *without* using the Force, but he knew his thoughts were pointless. He could not undo his actions.

"Now," Sidious said, "what did you wish to ask me earlier?"

Speaking tentatively, Maul said, "How long must I go on being one thing here and another there? Trained in the Force here, and trained to do without it there? What are your plans for me, Master? What *am* I to you?"

Sidious sniffed. "You are my student, Maul, and one day you may become my apprentice."

Despite all that his Master had taught him, Maul knew practically nothing about Sidious. How had Sidious obtained his wealth or gained so much knowledge of the Force? It was a mystery to Maul. For all he knew, Sidious was a warlord, a sorcerer, a monarch, or even a banished Jedi Master. Maul said flatly, "Your apprentice."

"Perhaps. But if that is meant to be, it will come at the end of many trials that will make these present ones seem insignificant. Removed from the shelter of Orsis, you will begin to understand that the Republic is built on deceit, and that it only survives because the Jedi Order wishes it to survive. You will need to be resolute in your allegiance to the dark side of the Force."

Maul nodded. "I understand, Master."

"No," Sidious said. "You only think you do." From the folds of his dark robe, he produced two lightsabers. He tossed one to Maul, then ignited the weapon that remained in his own hand.

Maul ignited his lightsaber. From the look in his Master's eyes, he guessed that the burns he was about to sustain would be much more painful than the ones he'd received from Meltch Krakko's blaster.

He guessed right.

A week later, most of Maul's wounds had healed as he prepared for the Gora. He was in the Academy barracks, modifying his combat vibroblade's ultrasonic vibration generator, when Kilindi and another female cadet, Daleen, walked in. Daleen was a dark-haired human, slightly younger than Kilindi, and rumor had it that she was the princess of a royal house.

Kilindi said, "Meltch came looking for you."

Maul glanced at the doorway. "Where is he now?"

"Up top, I think," Daleen said.

Maul knew "up top" meant Orsis Orbital Station. He also knew it wasn't unusual for Meltch Krakko to be there, that the Mandalorian instructor occasionally met with off-worlders at the station. But in the past week, Maul had begun to wonder if Sidious and Trezza had conspired against him, if they had encouraged Krakko to push him beyond his limits, all in an effort to find out whether Maul would break his agreement and use the Force. Now, he wondered if Sidious and Krakko ever crossed paths on Orsis Orbital.

Kilindi said, "Want any tips on what to watch out for in the Gora?"

Maul shook his head as he returned his attention to modifying his vibroblade. "I'll make do."

Kilindi laughed. "That's what *I* said, and look where it got me." Turning around, she shifted her head tentacles to display a relatively recent set of scars that crisscrossed her muscular arms and shoulders. Although bacta treatment would have erased all her scars, Kilindi kept them as proof of her experience.

Grinning at Maul, Daleen said, "Just don't get lost out there." She reached out and gently rubbed the back of his head, careful not to touch his horns. "We're cooking up a surprise for your return."

Kilindi and Daleen walked out of the barracks, leaving Maul wondering what they might be up to. Generally, Maul did not like surprises, as few in his life had been pleasant. But as much as he had been looking forward to the Gora, he now looked forward even more to seeing Kilindi and Daleen when the Gora was over.

The first day of the Gora was beyond intense.
The second day was even more brutal.

113

The third, fourth, fifth, and sixth days were increasingly bloody. And Maul was having the time of his life.

Countless wild predators kept him constantly occupied as well as sleepless. Except for his heightened senses and physical strength, he did not use the Force in any obvious way. With his vibroblade more often in his hand than in the sheath strapped to his upper leg, he moved like a jungle animal through the forests and grassy swamps that filled the enormous crater, killing some beasts in self-defense, some for food, and others for sheer sport.

Never had he known such freedom. After years of obeying others while containing his rage, he was able to run and hunt and kill as he pleased. By the seventh day, he almost regretted that his journey across the Gora would soon be over.

And then the storm hit. The clouds seemed to roll in from out of nowhere. Within minutes, torrential downpours and hurricane winds hammered at the jungle, turning ground to mud and tearing trees from the ground. The Gora had been dangerous enough with bloodthirsty creatures lurking everywhere, and Maul began to wonder if nature itself were trying to kill him.

Scrambling over fallen trees and trudging through flooded swamps, he made his way through a thorn forest to a rustic outpost, his final destination in the Gora. Once he reached the outpost, he could call for an airspeeder to return him to the Academy. He was eager to see Kilindi and Daleen again.

The storm began to die as Maul left the thorn forest and emerged at a broad savannah. He knew the outpost wasn't far, just beyond the grasslands that stretched out before him. But as he began to move across the savannah, he heard footfalls from the forest.

Llian beasts, he determined. Llians were large creatures with spined tails, and although they didn't travel in herds, it sounded as if at least three were heading straight for him. As he drew his vibroblade, he scanned the grasslands, searching for a length of wood so he might quickly improvise a lance. But no such wood or deadfall was in sight.

Four llians burst from the forest, and Maul was surprised to see each beast bore a rider. The riders were slim humanoids dressed in red, hooded garments. Each was armed with an energy bow and pike.

Maul did not recognize the riders, but knew at a glance they were formidable warriors. Although he felt the dark side of the Force swell within him, he did not summon his powers to defend himself. He suspected that Master Sidious had sent the warriors to test his loyalty and commitment.

The llians moved around Maul. Three warriors drew their energy bows and fired glowing arrows at Maul, not to strike him but to drive him back to the fourth mounted warrior who had moved up behind him. Maul dodged the arrows but was knocked backward by an invisible force, and then yanked off his feet so he was suspended upside down in the air a full meter above the ground. The vibroblade fell from his hand.

Inverted and immobilized, he saw the fourth warrior dismount. From his upside-down perspective, he saw a tall, silver-eyed female with a pale face that was adorned with angular black tattoos. Below her high-peaked red hood, a shieldlike hexagonal medallion appeared to be affixed to her unusually high forehead. A trove of talismans and amulets dangled around her thin neck. As she walked toward Maul, tapered streamers shifted behind her robe, moving like tendrils with a life of their own. "Don't resist, Nightbrother Maul," she said. Her voice was deep, with a most unusual accent.

Maul sensed the Force about her. He was certain she was in league with Sidious, possibly an apprentice. Before he could respond, she made a gesture with her hands and then extended one long finger to touch his forehead.

Maul plunged into unconsciousness.

He awoke groggily, feeling drained, as if he had been robbed of the Force. From the noise and vibrations around him, he knew he was inside a small spaceship. Shifting his fingers to his upper leg, he felt the empty sheath to confirm his vibroblade was gone.

He opened his eyes. He was lying on an accelerator chair in the main cabin of a drop ship. Pushing himself up, he saw the woman who had rendered him unconscious. Apparently, the woman and her fellow warriors were so confident in their strength that they had not bothered to cuff or shackle him.

"You are skilled, Maul," the woman said from her own seat, "but perhaps not as skilled as I was led to believe."

Maul sneered. "That seems to be the common opinion lately."

The woman's eyes widened slightly. "Very revealing. A few moments ago I was thinking that I erred in coming so far and in risking so much to return you to your clan brothers. And yet I sense that you are strong in the Force."

"I have no brothers," Maul said sharply, as if he found the word distasteful.

"Ah, but you do. And once among them your life will be very different. On Dathomir, you will be nurtured and trained as the Winged Goddess and the Fanged God meant you to be trained. When the time is right you will face the Nightbrothers' equivalents of the Tests of Fury, Night, and Elevation. And should you pass those trials, you may be fortunate enough to be transformed into an extraordinary warrior. Your strength will be enhanced tenfold, and those puny horns that stipple your head presently will become long and lethal."

Maul had stopped listening as soon as she'd mentioned Dathomir. Sidious had told him about the Nightsisters, the Force-using witches who ruled that world. He thought of his most recent meeting with his Master, a week prior to the Gora, when Sidious had cautioned him that "beings of all nature" would attempt to deceive him, to fill his head with lies. There was no question in his mind that the witch who had captured him was associated with Sidious, that she was either deliberately or unwittingly testing Maul. He refused to become a pawn in their game.

"I won't be going to Dathomir."

The witch raised an eyebrow. "You've no interest in seeing your birth world or meeting the members of your Nightbrother clan?"

"Neither."

The witch frowned. "You are fated to serve us, Maul, one way or the other. It has always been thus."

Staring hard at the witch, Maul said, "I serve only one Master."

The witch smiled without mirth. "The Falleen you answer to will have to find another."

The Falleen? Maul was confused. Was she under the impression that Trezza was his only Master, or was she toying with him? He considered mentioning Sidious by name, but decided against it.

A red-garbed Nightsister stepped into the cabin. She was armed with an energy bow and a sheathed energy sword, a fixed-blade weapon that resembled a glowing lightsaber. Maul recognized the Nightsister as one of the warriors who'd attacked him in the Gora. Like the seated witch, she had pale white skin and a tattooed face, but Maul noticed she was younger and did not have such a high forehead. The Nightsister said, "Mother Talzin, we are approaching the station."

Talzin nodded but kept her eyes on Maul. "Can I trust you to behave while we transfer to our vessel, or do you wish simply to awaken aboard it?"

Maul glanced at the young Nightsister's weapons. "For the moment, you have the upper hand. I won't make trouble."

"Of course you won't," Talzin said soothingly.

Maul looked out a viewport and saw they were approaching Orsis Orbital Station. A moment later, the drop ship shuddered as a tractor beam locked onto it. As the tractor beam eased the ship into one of the station's docking bays, Maul considered his limited options.

He knew that the station's cargo and passenger hubs were linked at several points by air lock corridors. If he could break away from the Nightsisters and get to another ship, he might be able to return to Orsis before anyone at the Academy realized he had left the Gora. He would prove to Sidious that he would not be taken so easily.

The drop ship touched down in the space station's large, dimly illuminated cargo bay. As Maul walked with Talzin and the three Nightsisters down the drop ship's boarding ramp, he was struck by a sudden feeling of apprehension. Talzin must have sensed something as well, because she turned to look at him, as if he might be the cause of her concern.

Maul said, "Trouble."

CHAPTER ELEVEN

Sensing he was being watched by hidden life-forms, Maul scanned the shadowy corners of the high-walled cargo bay. Without any prompting from Talzin, the three Nightsisters drew their swords and enabled their energy bows. Talzin stepped away from her group, moving out into the middle of the cargo bay as if she were not worried in the least.

"Stay right where you are and lower your weapons," a gruff voice barked from the cargo bay loudspeakers. And then the life-forms emerged from shadows. Leathery-skinned Weequays stood amongst large-headed Siniteens, all armed with blaster rifles that were leveled at Maul and the Nightsisters.

A towering figure clad from head to foot in garish battle armor moved to the center of the cutthroats. He was a Vollick, a native of Rattatak, an Outer Rim world infamous for its gladiatorial death matches. A remarkably large blaster was holstered to his hip.

Each of his arms looked as if they weighed more than Maul's body.

"You won't be returning to Dathomir, Mother Talzin," the Vollick said. "The five of you are going to be my guests on Rattatak, where you will eventually become members of my elite army." He drew his enormous blaster from its holster and fired a shot at the bay's tall ceiling. "Our weapons are set on stun, but we'll shoot to kill if you decide to refuse my invitation."

Maul wondered how the Vollick warlord and his soldiers had known Talzin would be arriving on the space station, and then he wondered if the Vollick might be Talzin's accomplice. Talzin said nothing. She raised her hands as if in surrender, then extended her fingers.

Maul was surprised to see dozens of Nightsister warriors materialize from the sidewalls and upper levels of the docking bay. However, he instantly sensed they were insubstantial, that the new arrivals were nothing more than a powerful Force illusion created by Talzin. The warlord and his soldiers fell for it. They rapidly reset their blasters' selector switches from stun to full power, angled their weapons away from Talzin, and opened fire at the apparitions. Genuine blaster bolts and illusory arrows began crisscrossing the bay.

The real Nightsisters drew their energy bows and began launching very real arrows at the Weequays and Siniteens. They dropped several soldiers before Talzin's conjured illusion evaporated unexpectedly.

Maul glanced at Talzin, saw her frustrated expression, and wondered if she had complete control of her powers.

"Cease fire!" yelled the startled Vollick. "Cease fire!" But his men ignored him and turned their weapons on the genuine Nightsisters who remained in the bay. As Maul ducked for cover, he saw a Weequay blast one of the Nightsisters at the same moment that a Siniteen fired a shot that tore through Talzin's thigh. The Nightsister dropped her energy bow as she collapsed. Talzin stumbled and fell on the deck several meters away from Maul.

Maul considered running back into the drop ship, but he doubted that it had sufficient power to escape the bay's tractor beam array. And looking at Talzin sprawled on the deck, he also began to wonder whether Sidious wanted her dead. He thought, *If this is a test, it's for keeps.*

He ran toward the fallen Nightsister, leaping and tumbling across the deck until he reached her energy bow. He didn't have to look at her to know she was dead. Snatching up her weapon, he darted back to the drop ship, took cover behind one of the landing struts, and began firing back at the warlord's men. Talzin was still lying on the deck. The two remaining Nightsisters had moved beside her and were unleashing a barrage of arrows at their opponents.

Maul scanned the cargo bay. Recalling the space station's layout from previous visits, he visualized the shortest route to a neighboring bay where he hoped to find another drop ship. He was still working with his rough plan to return to Orsis before anyone discovered he was missing. Although he would have accomplished this goal more easily if he used the Force, he did not want to disappoint his Master again. He was about to make a break for the nearest hatchway when he heard Talzin call out, "Don't leave us, Maul!"

Talzin was on her feet, supported by one of the Nightsisters while the other was covering them. Blaster bolts whizzed past them. Talzin cried, "Maul!"

Maul didn't know what to do. Would Sidious expect him to show sympathy? Was Talzin even one of Sidious's agents? Either way, how would he better serve the dark side of the Force? By helping the Nightsisters, or leaving them to die?

Maul cursed through his gritted teeth. He hooked the energy bow over his right shoulder, then ran through a hail of blaster bolts to reach Talzin. He heaved her up from the deck, flung her over his left shoulder, and raced for the entrance of a cylindrical corridor that led to the safety of an adjacent bay. The two Nightsisters followed, firing arrows at the warlord and his soldiers behind them as they moved after Maul.

Maul was fifty meters shy of the connector's entrance when a hail of blaster bolts cut him off. He carried Talzin behind a large cargo container for cover, then propped her up on the deck beside the container. The other two

Nightsisters arrived, positioned their bodies to protect Talzin, and returned fire. Maul looked at Talzin.

"Our magicks don't work in this sterile place," Talzin said bitterly as blaster bolts ricocheted off the container. "That's why I could not sustain the illusion."

"The illusion that nearly got all of us killed," Maul said.

Talzin winced as she moved her hand over the deep wound in her outer thigh. "On Dathomir, I would be able to heal myself."

"No one asked you to come here," Maul said, but then thought maybe she had responded to an invitation from Sidious.

"We came for your sake."

"That's a lie."

Talzin's silver eyes flared. "You fail to grasp that you belong to a great heritage, Maul. That you were spirited away from Dathomir doesn't alter the fact that you are a Nightbrother, and that your fate is joined with ours."

Maul snorted. "Everyone has a plan for me."

Talzin's brow furrowed, then she said, "I don't understand."

Maul ignored her as he tried to find a way out. Looking to the area between the cargo container and the soldiers, he saw a dozen automated load-lifter droids. Apparently oblivious to the firefight, the simple-minded droids were hauling similar cargo containers to different areas of the bay. The containers were drifting

125

slowly into the bay on powerful tractor beams from a cargo ship that was too large to be berthed inside the station. Maul knew enough about starship technology to know that a computer housed in the bay's upper-level control room was guiding the droids and tractor beams. Looking up, he found the control room's window.

"We've one chance to make it through the connector and into the passenger pod," Maul said. He looked at Talzin. "I'm going to need one of your energy swords."

"You've no training in the use of that weapon," said Talzin.

Maul shrugged the energy bow from his shoulder. "I'll just have to improvise."

Talzin grabbed an energy sword from one of the Nightsisters and handed it to Maul. Taking the sword, he leaped away from the cargo container, hit the deck, and then sprinted for the control room's bulkhead.

The soldiers turned their weapons and fired at Maul. Gripping the energy sword with both hands, he sprang from the deck, launching himself up toward the control room. He plunged the sword through the control room's window, creating a vertical hole, then flipped his body to kick the window and shatter it. As he landed inside the control room, the soldiers fired more blaster bolts after him, and the bolts ricocheted off the room's walls. One stray bolt grazed the side of Maul's upper right arm, drawing blood.

Ignoring the pain, Maul dropped to the control room's floor until he reached the main control board. His education at Orsis Academy had included learning how to override computers, and he quickly reprogrammed the cargo bay's tractor beam array.

Almost instantly, the cargo containers that had been drifting slowly into the bay were suddenly soaring in at rapid speed. Although the increased speed had no effect on the cargo ship parked outside the space station, the containers began piling up inside the bay faster than the load-lifter droids could catch them. The pile quickly accumulated into a wall of containers that separated the soldiers from the Nightsisters, but left the Nightsisters with a clear passage to the connector that led to the space station's passenger hub.

Rising from the control room's floor, Maul glanced down to see several soldiers trying to run to the far side of the bay before the incoming containers cut them off. The containers moved faster than the soldiers could run, and they were crushed. The remaining soldiers retreated.

Maul jumped down from the control room and returned to Talzin and the two Nightsisters. He wrapped his arm around Talzin's waist and helped her to her feet. The Nightsisters followed Maul and Talzin into the air lock corridor.

With the Nightsisters bringing up the rear, the two of them hurried to the entrance of the cylindrical corridor.

Maul saw the entrance's sealed hatch, but because he didn't want to lose his hold on Talzin, he used the Force to open the hatch. After they all moved through the hatch and into the corridor's first airlock, Talzin used the Force to seal the hatch behind them, and the pair of Nightsisters launched their energy quarrels to destroy the hatch's control panel. An alarm began blaring. Maul ignored it and kept moving.

Working as a team, they repeated their actions as they moved through several more hatches until they reached the station's passenger hub. Maul wasn't sure what Sidious would think of his use of the Force, but as they moved into the passenger hub, he became absolutely certain that his Master was testing him. He was so certain that he stopped in his tracks.

"Why are you waiting?" Talzin said. "Our ship isn't that far."

"You can stop pretending," Maul said.

Apparently confused, Talzin shook her head. "About what?"

"About Dathomir, the Nightbrothers, and the rest. I know that you were sent by my Master. I know, because I sense him. My Master is here."

Moving through a maintenance level to avoid more soldiers, Maul, Talzin, and the Nightsisters finally arrived in the hangar that housed Talzin's starship. Maul had expected to find the warlord's soldiers stationed in the hangar to prevent Talzin from reaching her ship, but he had not expected to find over a dozen Weequays lying dead on the hangar's deck.

Although none of the Weequay bodies bore obvious wounds, Maul knew how they had died, and also the identity of their killer. Leaving Talzin standing with her Nightsisters, he moved across the hangar to face a dark alcove. He stopped, dropped to one knee, and bowed his head.

"Master."

Sidious stepped out from the alcove. He wore his dark robe, and his face was concealed by the shadows beneath his deep hood.

Talzin and the Nightsisters fell back a step. Evidently, they could sense the man's power in the dark side of the Force. As the Nightsisters kept their energy bows aimed at the deck, Sidious turned slightly toward them, gestured to Maul, and said, "This one does not belong to Dathomir. He is mine."

Talzin said, "Then you didn't merely abandon him to the Falleen."

"On the contrary," Sidious said.

Talzin glanced at Maul. "You have trained him well."

Sidious motioned to Talzin's ship. "You'll find the body of your fallen Nightsister aboard."

Talzin nodded her head in gratitude. Sidious folded his hands into the opposite sleeves of his robe and said, "Now, be gone from here before I have a change of mind."

Talzin was unaccustomed to taking orders, but she gestured to the Nightsisters to board the ship. The Nightsisters walked past Maul, who was still kneeling with his head lowered. As Talzin limped past Maul, she casually allowed her dangling left hand to brush the bloody wound that had been opened in his upper right arm. She proceeded up the boarding ramp. Neither Maul nor Sidious noticed her move her left hand to one of the talismans that dangled from her neck, and press Maul's blood upon the talisman before she entered her ship.

Talzin's ship lifted from the deck and glided out of the hangar. Sidious moved to an observation window that overlooked Orsis. Maul followed obediently, then dropped to a kneeling posture and waited for his Master to speak.

Staring out the window, Sidious said at last, "You did well, Maul. It pleases me that you showed restraint and betrayed none of your training in the dark side of the Force."

Maul bowed his head. "I did so in the hope of one day becoming your apprentice."

Sidious glanced back at Maul. "Then consider yourself one step closer."

"Thank you, Master."

Sidious stepped away from the window. "The time has come for you to learn certain things about the nature of our undertaking. As I told you, I have been putting into motion the stages of a Grand Plan, a plan you may play a part in if you can continue to demonstrate worthiness and loyalty. You should know, though, that this plan has in fact been in the making for a millennium. It springs from the minds of many who serve a great tradition." He paused to look at Maul. "A tradition of far greater import than the Dathomiri brotherhood Talzin surely told you about. It is the tradition of the ancient order known as the Sith."

Surprised, Maul narrowed his eyes. "You told me of the Sith when I was young, Master."

"What I kept from you then is that I am the Sith Lord, *Darth* Sidious. My Master both named and conferred the title on me, and at my discretion, you may one day be afforded the same honor by me."

Maul swallowed hard. "I will strive to prove my worth to you, Master."

"Yes, you will," Sidious said. "From this point on I will begin to tutor you in the ways of the Sith. We are opponents of the Republic, and the sworn enemies of the Jedi Order. It will be our task to see the former brought down and the latter expunged from the galaxy. Where I will remain the guiding hand in this, it will fall to you to execute missions that could pose a risk to my position should the true purpose of our acts be discovered."

For years, Maul had wondered the purpose of all his training. Now he knew. His heart pounded.

"Nothing less than perfection will be sufficient, Maul," Sidious said. "Do you understand?"

Maul bowed his head again. "I understand, Master."

"Then let's put that to the test, shall we?"

Maul looked up. "Another?"

Sidious's brow furrowed. "Another?"

"As you engineered with Mother Talzin?"

Sidious grinned faintly. "What happened on Orsis and aboard this station was not set in motion by my hand, Maul. In fact, you were betrayed by one who told Talzin where to find you, and then aided and abetted her plan to capture you."

Maul's eyes widened with surprise, and then he felt a wave of anger. "May I know the identity of my betrayer, Master?"

Sidious looked at the ceiling for a moment as he considered Maul's request, then replied, "Meltch Krakko."

Krakko?! Maul scowled, wondering how long the Mandalorian had been plotting against him. "Did Trezza know, Master?"

Sidious shook his head. "Trezza knew nothing. However, I fear that we may not be able to contain the damage that has been done. We can't risk that word of your disappearance and all that followed may spread." He stroked his chin thoughtfully. "I will deal with the Vollick warlord. But it will be your task to deal with Trezza and the others at the school."

The others? Maul thought of Trezza, who had

always treated him with a degree of respect that Sidious never had. He thought of Kilindi and Daleen, who had shown him kindness. And then his pounding heart turned to stone and he said, "I live to do your bidding, Master."

Sidious nodded. "And as long as you do, you will continue to live."

Maul rose.

"Be discreet," Sidious said.

Leaving the space station, Maul traveled by drop ship back down to Orsis. On his way, he visualized what he had to do. He knew the layout for every building at the Academy, knew every entrance and exit. He thought of all the things he hated about the place, especially the rules that forbade him from using the Force.

Night had long fallen by the time he reached the Academy's perimeter, and he felt very different from the cadet he had been when he left to begin the Gora. Now, his education seemed ages behind him. He felt he was one with the dark side of the Force.

He moved quickly and quietly through the courtyards and buildings. First, he killed the Academy's sentries, and then the security guards posted outside the training rooms and barracks. He used the Force when it was most efficient, and his bare hands whenever it pleased him. Knowing that most of the cadets would already be asleep in the barracks, he went noiselessly from one darkened room to the next, leaving a trail of death.

He entered the room shared by Kilindi and Daleen. Kilindi's bunk was empty. Daleen's wasn't. Daleen was snoring lightly. A moment later, her life had ended, and Maul was moving out the door. He took no comfort from Kilindi's absence. He knew he would find her.

When he arrived upon the sleeping forms of the Rodians Hubnutz and Fretch, he woke them before he broke their necks.

Not every cadet was sleeping. Maul found a group of older cadets practicing martial arts in a training room. He locked the doors, switched off the lights, and moved through the group like a furious beast of prey.

Covered in blood, he proceeded to the building where the instructors had their own quarters.

Approaching the door to Trezza's office, he heard voices inside. He recognized the voices. Kilindi and Trezza. Kilindi was demanding that Trezza explain why Maul had not returned from the Gora. She sounded worried and angry. But as far as Maul was concerned, she was talking about someone else, someone he didn't know.

Maul opened the door and stepped into the office. Trezza was seated behind his massive desk. Kilindi stood before him. And Meltch Krakko stood on the far side of the room, near an open fireplace.

Kilindi gasped at the sight of Maul's blood-soaked

body. Maul fixed his gaze on Krakko and walked straight toward him. Even though Maul was not carrying any weapons, Krakko drew his blaster and fired at him. Maul jerked his body to the left, dodged the blaster bolt, and kept walking toward Krakko. Krakko fired two more shots. Maul dodged those too before he grabbed Krakko's gun arm with one hand, and his neck with the other. Krakko sputtered angrily. What Maul did next made Trezza gasp and Kilindi cover her mouth with her hands.

Maul kept his eyes on Trezza as he hurled Krakko's lifeless body into the fireplace. Trezza raised his hands to show he wasn't holding any weapons and said, "Maul, please calm yourself. We can talk about this." Keeping his hands raised, he looked anxiously at Kilindi.

Maul sensed Trezza's anxiety and knew Trezza was just trying to stall and distract him. He was not surprised to see the flat metal knife pop out of Trezza's sleeve.

Catching the knife between his fingers, Trezza threw it at Maul. Maul's left hand flew in front of him to catch the knife by its handle, then whipped it back with blinding speed at Trezza's upper chest. Trezza gasped, clutched at his chest, and collapsed upon his desk.

Maul looked at Kilindi. She was staring at him blankly, but she radiated fear like a child in the presence of an enormous monster. Maul walked toward her. He never paused to wonder how his life might have been different if he had not revealed his Force powers to Meltch

Krakko. He never paused at all. His only purpose was to serve his Master.

Kilindi didn't run. She did try to smile. She said, "I guess you're not interested in the surprise that Daleen and I had for you."

"Not anymore," Maul said.

Soon after the destruction of Orsis Academy, Maul learned why Sidious had been so protective of his own identity for so many years. Evidently, Sidious had long maintained another identity as a public figure, a Senator from the planet Naboo. In his Senatorial guise on the planet Coruscant and other worlds throughout the Galactic Republic, Sidious was known as Palpatine. Most people who knew Palpatine regarded him as a polite, quiet man, as modest as he was harmless.

Maul moved with Sidious to Coruscant, where Sidious had long kept a secret lair in a skyscraper in an industrial area. Maul spent the next two years carrying out a series of secret missions for his Master. The missions were conceived to help Sidious gain power without others ever knowing of his existence. By the end of those two years, Maul had repeatedly proven that he was as strong as he was fast, and that he would never break. He also sensed that his control of the darkness that fueled the Force was close to perfect.

CHAPTER TWELVE

Sidious and Maul returned to Mustafar. For fourteen days, Sidious put Maul through a series of grueling physical tests. Maul defended himself against lightsaber-wielding droids in the training room. Blindfolded, he threw daggers at robotic targets, which threw the daggers back at him. He was blindfolded again before he climbed into a starship flight simulator wired with disciplinary electrodes. He wore a sensory-deprivation suit when he ran through a maze that was lined with razor-edged walls, and also when he was deposited into a previously unexplored Mustafarian cave. In locked chambers, he was exposed to extreme temperatures and deprived of food. For each test, he drew strength from the dark side of the Force.

When the fourteen days were over, Maul was exhausted. His entire body ached as he stood before Sidious in the meeting room. Not only had he passed every test, he had destroyed every test. However, his

Master always expected more from him, so he was not entirely surprised when Sidious said, "Because you have survived the preliminaries, you may proceed to the actual test to become a Sith Lord."

Maul willed his body to remain standing.

"I am sending you to a planet in the Outer Rim," Sidious continued. "It is made up of three kinds of terrain. Desert, swamp, and mountains. You will have at least three matches on each terrain. I have sent a fleet of assassin droids to attack you. Each is programmed with different strategies. Some will work together. Some will work alone. They are all programmed to kill."

Maul turned to face his Master. Although Maul remained silent, the fire in his eyes betrayed his surprise. And his excitement.

Sidious noticed Maul's reaction. "That is correct. I am prepared to lose what I most value. So must you be to become a Sith. You must be prepared to lose your own life in order to win."

Maul nodded. "I understand, my Master."

"You will have to survive for a month," Sidious added. "You will have only a survival pack."

Despite his exhaustion, Maul felt exhilarated. He was determined to prove he was the best apprentice in the history of the Sith.

Sidious did not accompany Maul in the droid-piloted cruiser that left Mustafar, nor did he inform Maul of the cruiser's destination. But while the cruiser was traveling through hyperspace, Maul tapped at a keypad at the navigation console until he accessed and bypassed the coded coordinates that identified his destination as Hypori, a planet in the Ferra sector of the Outer Rim Territories. He had never been to Hypori before, but he had not expected his Master to send him to a familiar world.

The droid pilot emerged from the cockpit and noticed Maul examining a scope at the navigation console. The droid said, "I don't think Master Sidious will be pleased to know that you accessed restricted data from the navicomputer."

Without looking away from the scope, Maul replied, "When Master Sidious learns that you used dated encryption codes for the destination coordinates, he'll feed you through a shredder for a full week."

"Oh," said the droid pilot. "If you'll excuse me, I'm going to erase my memory of the past minute."

Good idea, Maul thought as the droid returned to the cockpit. But then it occurred to him that the droid pilot might actually be an assassin droid. He could only imagine how many assassin droids were already waiting for him on Hypori, and it was possible that the pilot droid would deliver him straight into a massive ambush.

The cruiser dropped out of hyperspace to arrive within view of Hypori. It was a small world, and scattered clouds were visible in the upper atmosphere. Even from space, Maul could make out some wide areas of desert, small oceans, and shadowy mountain ranges, which were consistent with Sidious's description of the varied terrain.

The cruiser descended through the planet's atmosphere. Maul grabbed the survival pack that Sidious had given to him and strapped it to his back. He leaned into the cockpit, looked through the window, and saw they were angling down over a body of water, heading toward a rocky beach.

The droid swiveled its mechanical eyes to face Maul and said, "Please don't ask me where we're going to land. I'm not authorized to tell you."

Ignoring the droid, Maul examined the ship's readouts for flight speed and altitude, then cast a final glance through the window, noting the distance to the beach, before he pulled out of the cockpit. As he mentally calculated the cruiser's approach to the beach, he dropped to a crouch beside the main hatch, wrapped one arm tightly around his legs so his knees were clasped against his chest, and used his free hand to hit the lever for the emergency exit.

The hatch exploded open. Maul kept his head pressed against his knees as he sailed out of the cruiser, fifty-five meters above sea level. He tumbled through the air, the cruiser's engines whining away from him as it veered across the sky. Automatically recalculating his descent, he twisted at the waist before he straightened and extended his legs skyward. His fists braced before him, he knifed into the water.

The water was cold. Holding his breath, Maul made sure the survival pack was still secured against his back, then began swimming to shore, staying below the water's surface. He suspected the droid pilot would tell Sidious about his leap from the cruiser, but that did not concern him. His test required that he survive for a month on Hypori. Sidious had never told him to remain on the cruiser until it landed.

When Maul neared the shore, he broke the surface with his mouth and nose but kept his body underwater. He reached out with his senses. He could not detect any movement on the rocky beach, but he knew it was only a matter of time before the assassin droids found him.

And then they found him.

The assassin droids were relentless. Programmed to fight to the death, they had blasters built into their chests and hands. No matter how hard Maul tried to conceal himself or his desperately improvised camps, the droids found him. They never slept, never allowed Maul to sleep for very long, never hesitated before they pounced. When Maul did manage to rest and recover, he fell asleep *knowing* he would be awakened by an attack.

The droids drove him into the frozen mountains and across the burning deserts. Maul's survival pack was torn from his back and lost in one battle. And after twenty days, Maul realized he was at risk of losing something else. His mind.

Because the attacks never stopped.

Maul was beyond paranoid. He had reason to believe that every sound, every shape, and every shadow on Hypori was a potential threat.

He grew thin and his strength began to ebb. He foraged for food when he could. Life was scarce on Hypori, but he found a few small animals, killed them, and ate them raw, because he dared not risk building a fire that would attract more droids.

It was while he was trying to eat a tough-skinned lizard at the base of a cliff that two droids attacked. Maul defeated both droids but sustained a blaster wound to his thigh. Limping into a ravine, he found a large cave and hauled his body into it. Maul knew he had to recover before he could fight again. But without his survival pack, he had no healing bacta or bandages.

The wound festered. The pain was blinding. He listened for approaching droids but heard none. The days blurred, but Maul was almost certain that a full month had passed since he had arrived on Hypori. As he fell into and out of restless sleep, Maul began to wonder if his Master had forgotten him.

His wound became worse. The pain was beyond excruciating. He had no doubt that death would come soon. He thought he was hallucinating when he saw a cloaked figure appear at the mouth of the cave.

It was Sidious.

Maul could not believe his eyes. He felt not only relieved to see his Master, but genuinely glad. His Master would help him.

Sidious moved into the cave. He came to a stop near Maul. Smiling as he looked down at his apprentice, he said, "Now it is time for your final battle."

Maul wondered if he had heard correctly. He knew his Master must have been able to see plainly that he was not fit to stand. And yet he also knew his Master never tolerated weakness of any kind. Maul scrabbled at the cave's walls and pulled himself up. His balance was off. Searing pain shot through his leg as he lurched forward.

Sidious handed Maul a lightsaber. Maul fumbled with the weapon and activated it. The cave's walls shimmered with light.

Maul did not realize how parched his throat was until he rasped, "Where is the assassin droid, Master?"

Stepping back from Maul, Sidious drew his own lightsaber and ignited its red blade. "I will be your opponent."

Maul stared at his Master with disbelief. And then his disbelief changed to anger. He summoned up the dark side of the Force. He felt a burning sensation flicker and grow within him, a trickle of strength. He took a step toward his Master.

Sidious sneered. "You cannot be as pathetic as you look." He raised his lightsaber and attacked.

Maul parried the blow and reversed, coming at Sidious from the opposite side. But Sidious had already vanished, leaving Maul to lunge at empty air. As Maul lost his balance, his body fell against the cave's wall.

Sidious said from behind Maul, "You *are* that pathetic. You are weak. Not worthy of being a Sith Lord. I have misjudged you."

Maul's anger turned to rage. He spun fast and swung his lightsaber again, but again he failed to strike Sidious, who moved faster than he could follow. He fell against the opposite wall and gasped for breath.

Sidious howled with laughter. "I expected your failure. I saw your weaknesses long ago. Your doubts in your own abilities. Your *lack of faith* in my teaching. Your *inability* to embrace the dark side. And that is why, over these long years, I have secretly trained another apprentice."

Maul stared hard at Sidious.

"Oh, poor Maul. All he ever wanted was a friend. Does it please you to know I have another apprentice? Does it make you feel less alone?"

Still trying to catch his breath, Maul said, "More than one apprentice . . . is against the rules of the Sith."

"You are right," Sidious said with a grin. "A spark of intelligence, at last." He gestured to the mouth of the cave. "My second apprentice is on the other side of the planet. He conquered all the assassin droids sent after him. He only sustained a flesh wound. He is healthy. He is strong. Unlike the pathetic weakling I see before me."

Maul realized his opponents had not really been the assassin droids. He thought of all the punishment he had endured over the past month, and then of the unending punishments of his entire life. He thought of his true opponent, the unseen adversary, chosen by Sidious to become a Sith Lord. Maul felt robbed of his past and future. And then a rage unlike anything he had ever felt before swelled through him. The rage was so overwhelming that he thought it might consume him.

No. I can direct it. My rage will consume my enemy. It will consume my Master. Glaring at Sidious, Maul saw the true face of his enemy.

Sidious snickered. "Can you understand? Focus. If there can be only one apprentice, then one of you must die. Who do you think I have chosen to die, Maul?"

Maul felt his rage flowing through his veins, pumping energy into every muscle. He felt so powerful that he believed he could accomplish anything. And more than anything else, he wanted his Master's blood.

Maul sprang at Sidious. Sidious barely missed the first blow from Maul's lightsaber, an upward swing that aimed to rip Sidious in half. Maul swung again but Sidious deflected the blow and retreated. As Maul moved across the rough cave floor, sweat stung his eyes, but he did not stumble. He somersaulted through the air, his lightsaber whirling in the darkness. Sidious raised his lightsaber to parry the next blow, which was so powerful it made him stagger backward. As Maul struck again, he thought, *I'm going to kill him.*

Sidious parried every blow, but Maul could tell his Master was working hard to keep him at bay. As Sidious backed up against the wall, he said, "You want to kill me? You want to kill your Master?"

"Yes," Maul grunted.

"You hate me?"

"Yes!" Maul screamed through clenched teeth.

Sidious shifted like a liquid shadow, maneuvering around his apprentice. Maul was suddenly up against the wall, gasping for breath as his vision blurred. His strength was evaporating. He turned fast to see Sidious. Sidious lashed out with his lightsaber. Maul parried the blow, but then his lightsaber suddenly flew from his hand.

As Maul heard his lightsaber deactivate and clatter across the cave's floor, Sidious raised his own lightsaber and advanced. Maul knew he was about to die, but he did not cringe. As Sidious swung his lightsaber, Maul leaped forward, grabbed Sidious's wrist, and sank his teeth into his hand. Maul tasted blood and spat it back at Sidious.

Sidious brought the lightsaber down on Maul. Maul waited for the pain and the shock of death.

He was surprised when the lightsaber's blade bounced off his shoulder.

Sidious cackled merrily. He stood and looked at Maul. Then he tossed the lightsaber aside. Maul realized his Master had been using a harmless training saber.

Maul leaned back against the cave wall. The rock bit into his back but he concentrated on the pain while his Master continued to laugh without mercy. When Sidious was done, he faced Maul and said, "Do you feel the hate?"

Maul nodded.

"Good. It is the source of your strength. You still hate me. No matter. Today you have delivered yourself into my hands. I have the power of life or death over you, Maul. Someday you will hold that power over another. It is the honor of the Sith. You will devote yourself to the idea of domination."

"But . . . what about the other apprentice?"

"There is no other apprentice."

Maul was astonished. He didn't know what to say.

"You have passed the test."

Maul could still taste his Master's blood on his lips, but his rage was rapidly ebbing. He shifted his feet and realized he was standing on his lost lightsaber. He picked it up and shoved it into his belt.

"From this day forward," Sidious said, "you are a Sith Lord. You have chosen a path of darkness, the path of power. You are Lord Maul. You are my instrument."

"Yes, Master."

Sidious smiled proudly. "Your rage. You enjoyed it? You enjoyed wanting to kill me?"

"I took pleasure in it."

Sidious laughed again, but it was not a mocking laughter. "You will do well, Lord Maul."

Maul realized he no longer felt any anger toward Sidious. He felt only . . . loyalty.

Sidious and Maul returned to Coruscant, where a medical droid tended to Maul's injuries. Maul had felt drained by his trials on Hypori, but within several days, he felt stronger than ever before. Now that he was a Sith Lord, he was empowered by a sense of purpose.

He was fully recovered when Sidious summoned him to his private library. He found Sidious examining an ancient pyramidal holocron. Maul knew from his studies that the holocron was a Sith artifact, used to preserve data.

Sidious glanced at his apprentice. "You are a formidable warrior, Lord Maul. Now you need a weapon to match. I have spent many hours perusing the Sith archives, and I believe I have found something appropriate for your fighting skills." He brushed his fingers along one edge of the holocron, and a moment later, the holocron projected a hologram of a double-ended lightsaber.

Maul stared at the hologram, fascinated by the weapon's appearance. Imagining the damage it would inflict, he suddenly felt eager to wield such a lightsaber.

"This will be your weapon, Lord Maul. In order to serve me well, you must be invincible." Pointing to the hologram, he continued, "You must build the lightsaber yourself so that you know it intimately. It will be fitted for your hand, balanced for your stroke. You shall train with it until it is a part of you. And then you shall join me on the greatest mission of all."

"What is that, Master?"

"The domination of the entire galaxy."

CHAPTER THIRTEEN

a visit

Maul was exercising in his training room on Coruscant and had just completed a triple backward flip when he heard the signal on his comlink. He pressed a button on the comlink and heard his Master's voice. "Strategy room. Now."

Maul strode fast to a turbolift and ascended to his Master's strategy-and-communications room. Maul suspected his Master wanted to give him an update about his plan that involved the Neimoidian Trade Federation.

Although Maul did not know every detail of his Master's current project, he was aware that Sidious had established an alliance with the greedy Neimoidians. The Neimoidians were angry because the Galactic Senate had imposed taxation on the former Free Trade Zones of the Republic's outlying star systems, but then Sidious told the Neimoidians how they could force an end to the new regulations, allowing them to reap even greater profits. Sidious had instructed the Neimoidians to use their battleships to form a blockade around the planet Naboo, and then deploy battle droids to invade the world. After the invasion, the Neimoidians would force Queen Amidala to sign a treaty with the Trade Federation, a treaty that would convince the Republic Senate that the Neimoidians had assumed control of Naboo legally. Maul trusted that this project was part of a larger scheme, and that his Master would explain everything in time.

Exiting the turbolift, Maul found Sidious waiting in the center of the strategy room, in front of the holocomm station. Sidious was wearing his robe with the hood draped across his back. He did not look pleased.

"The Neimoidians are signaling me," Sidious said, the irritation evident in his voice. "I want you to hear the transmission." Raising his hood to conceal his face, he continued, "No doubt they have contacted me because of some ridiculous setback that has sent them into a panic. Stay out of sight."

Maul moved to the side, stepping into a shadowy alcove near the comm console.

Maul watched as holograms of two Neimoidians materialized in the air before Sidious. Humanoids with lumpy grayish-green flesh and eyes with horizontal irises, the Neimoidians were Viceroy Nute Gunray, the leader of the Trade Federation, and Daultay Dofine, the captain of the Trade Federation's flagship vessel. Nute was distinguished by a tall, crested tiara. Daultay's head was topped by a command officer's gray miter, and his face wore an especially worried expression.

Sidious said, "What is it?"

"This scheme of yours has failed, Lord Sidious," Daultay replied, trembling. "We dare not go against these Jedi."

Jedi?! Maul saw his Master stiffen in anger, and then another hologram appeared in the air. Transmitted by the Neimoidians, the hologram showed a pair of Jedi—a bearded Jedi Master and his younger Padawan apprentice—seated in a meeting room in the Neimoidians' battleship.

Sidious sneered as he said, "Viceroy, I don't want this stunted slime in my sight again."

The cowardly Daultay ducked and shuffled out of view. Still facing Nute Gunray, Sidious continued, "This turn of events is unfortunate. We must accelerate our plans. Begin landing your troops."

Nute gasped. "My lord, is that . . . legal?"

"I will *make it* legal."

Nute's lumpy brow furrowed. "And the Jedi?"

"The Chancellor should never have brought them into this. Kill them immediately."

"Yes. Yes, my lord," Nute said hesitantly. "Uh . . . as you wish."

Sidious broke the connection and the holograms faded out. A question formed in Maul's mind. He knew that he should remain silent, that to interrupt his

Master's thoughts almost always brought harsh consequences. Unable to wait, Maul said, "Do you think the Neimoidians are capable of destroying the Jedi, Master? They are fools."

Sidious nodded slowly. "Yes, they are fools. But even fools are sometimes lucky."

Maul returned to his training room. He moved his hand over a sensor on a curved wall, and then the wall panel slid back to offer a sweeping view of Coruscant. The city appeared to spread out above, below, and around Maul. The sun was setting, and he watched the sky shift to crimson. As millions of gleaming windows and passing starships reflected the color of the sky, Maul thought the entire world looked as if it were bathed in blood. He thought it was beautiful.

And then he thought of the two Jedi who had arrived at the Neimoidians' blockade at Naboo. He hoped the Neimoidians would fail to kill the Jedi. By the Force, he *knew* they would fail. And after all his years of training, he would be called into service to strike against the Sith's greatest enemy.

Maul grimaced. He realized that by wishing for the Neimoidians to fail, he was also wishing for his Master's order to fail. Maul did not like this contradiction, the conflict it presented. He did not want to be disloyal, but he couldn't stop the feeling that gnawed within him. . . .

The Jedi are mine. Mine to hunt. Mine to destroy.

The feeling wasn't purely selfish. Maul wanted his Master to see that he was a worthy apprentice. As far as Maul was concerned, all his previous tests had been trivial. To fight the Jedi would be his first true test. The *ultimate* test.

From Maul's vantage point in Sidious's lair, the Jedi Temple was not visible. He closed his eyes and visualized the Temple in his mind and saw a smoking ruin. The bodies of fallen Jedi Knights and their small Padawans littered the stairwells and hallways. He saw himself standing in the rubble, surrounded by Jedi corpses. He envisioned his Master arriving to meet him at the scene.

Here is what I have done for you, Master.

I am pleased, Lord Maul.

Maul opened his eyes. His vision had been so realistic he could smell the blend of rising smoke and spilled blood. He had no doubt that he had seen something more than a dream. He knew he had glimpsed the future.

It wasn't long before Sidious once again summoned Maul to his strategy room. When Maul arrived, he found his Master wearing a quilted blue cloak with Naboo-style bloused sleeves. Sidious shrugged out of the cloak and donned his dark hooded robe.

With his face lost in shadows beneath the hood, he glanced at Maul as he gestured to the dark alcove a short distance behind the single seat at the communications console. "Stand over there," Sidious said. "Remain in the background. I may need you. Who knows what those Neimoidian slugs have managed to bungle this time?"

Sidious seated himself in front of the holoprojector and initiated a transmission to Nute Gunray's battleship. Maul watched from the dark alcove as a hologram of Nute and his diplomatic attaché Rune Haako materialized in the air before Sidious.

Eyeing the two Neimoidians, Sidious said, "What is your report of the invasion?"

"We control all the cities in the North," Nute replied, "and are searching for any other settlements."

"And Queen Amidala, has she signed the treaty?"

"She has disappeared, my lord," Nute said ruefully. "One Naboo cruiser got past the blockade."

Sidious snarled. "I want that treaty signed."

"My lord, it's impossible to locate the ship. It's out of our range."

"Not for a Sith," Sidious said. With a discreet motion of his hand that only Maul could see, Sidious gestured for Maul to approach. Maul stepped forward so he stood just behind his Master. He braced his arms across his chest and stared down at the Neimoidians' holograms.

Sidious continued, "This is my apprentice, Darth Maul. He will find your lost ship."

Maul saw the look of surprise and dismay on the faces of both Nute and Rune Haako as they shifted their gazes from Sidious to him. He thought, *Yes, you fools. There are two of us.*

Sidious broke the connection with the Neimoidians. Turning to face Maul, he said, "Those incompetents have performed worse than my lowest expectations. Queen Amidala *must* sign that treaty." He clenched his teeth. "The Jedi are behind this, of course. They are becoming a nuisance and must be eliminated. Find them."

Maul bowed. "I will find them, Master. I will not fail."

Sio Bibble, the governor of Naboo and chair of the Naboo Royal Advisory Council, was among the many citizens captured by the Neimoidians during the invasion of Naboo. Maul scavenged holographic datatapes to replicate Sio Bibble's likeness and voice and created a fragmented message from the white-haired, bearded governor. Reviewing the message, Maul watched Bibble's simulated likeness say urgently, ". . . cut off all food supplies until you return. The death toll is catastrophic. We must bow to their wishes. You must contact me."

Maul's plan was to transmit the message and establish a connection trace to pinpoint the location of Queen Amidala's starship. He routed the transmission so it would appear to originate from the Royal Palace on Naboo. And then he waited.

It did not take long for Maul to intercept a response, a brief encrypted message that said the Queen was safe and would soon return to Naboo. The response came from a small sand planet in the Arkanis sector, in the Outer Rim Territories. The planet's name was Tatooine.

Maul found Darth Sidious standing on a balcony that curved around the outside of their secret lair on Coruscant. Sidious was apparently oblivious to the airships that whizzed past the balcony as he gazed out over the skyscrapers that illuminated the night. As Maul approached, he heard his Master mutter . . .

"Far above, far above,
We don't know where we'll fall.
Far above, far above,
What once was great is rendered small."

Sidious glanced at Maul. Maul recalled the verse from his childhood and wondered why his Master had recited it, but he did not ask.

Sidious began walking on the balcony and Maul fell into step alongside him. Maul said, "A connection trace suggests the Queen is on Tatooine. She might be hiding there while she plans to retake her planet."

Sidious shook his head. "She is not so brave. She still trusts the power of the Senate. No, that is not why they landed on Tatooine. And the reason is not your concern. Just find them."

"Tatooine is sparsely populated," Maul said. "If the trace was correct, I will find them quickly, Master."

"Move against the Jedi first. You will then have no difficulty taking the Queen to Naboo to sign the treaty."

Sidious came to a stop at the edge of the balcony. Maul stopped beside him and said, "At last we will reveal ourselves to the Jedi. At last we will have revenge."

"You have been well trained, my apprentice. They will be no match for you."

Leaving his Master on the balcony, Maul proceeded to the hangar that housed his personal starship, the Sith Infiltrator named *Scimitar*. Sidious had given him the vessel, which was equipped with a powerful hyperdrive, weapons, and a rare cloaking device that rendered the ship completely invisible. Maul had used the ship on numerous missions on behalf of his Master, including recent attacks on the interstellar criminal organization Black Sun and Bartokk assassins on the planet Ralltiir.

After boarding the ship, he entered Tatooine's coordinates into the starship's navicomputer to plot his course through hyperspace, a course that would have him leave Coruscant via the Corellian Run and then shift to the Triellus Trade Route to reach Tatooine's binary star system in the Arkanis sector. Minutes later, seated behind the *Scimitar*'s controls, he was rising away from Coruscant when he realized his entire body was tingling with excitement.

He could hardly wait to kill Jedi.

CHAPTER FOURTEEN

a visit to tatoing

   The *Scimitar* dropped out of hyperspace. Maul glanced through a shielded viewport to see the twin suns of the Tatoo system, then spotted a third point of light that was so bright it could have easily been mistaken for a small star. Maul checked the nav console and confirmed the third body was Tatooine.

Although Maul did not expect to spend much time on the sand planet, he had briefed himself about what he would find there. The Republic had no functional presence on Tatooine, which was essentially run by the Hutts, large sluglike beings whose criminal enterprises spanned the galaxy. Because water on Tatooine was so scarce, most colonists were moisture farmers. Indigenous natives included bright-eyed Jawas, hooded scavengers who drove enormous sandcrawlers through the desert in search of scrap metal and abandoned vehicles. There were also nomadic masked savages called the Tusken Raiders, known to moisture farmers as Sand People, who rode large creatures called banthas. From what Maul had gathered about the Sand People, he doubted that Queen Amidala and the Jedi would seek refuge with them. Everyone avoided Sand People.

A light flashed on the comm console. The *Scimitar* had picked up a distress signal from a nearby ship. Maul sighted the ship on his viewscreen, saw it was a small space cruiser that had stalled in a shipping lane. He ignored the distress signal, but as he passed by the ship, the signal grew louder, and then a voice cried from the comm, "Help us! Please, help us!"

Maul saw a large bulk freighter tumble out of hyperspace, and he assumed the freighter had arrived to assist the stalled ship. But then the stalled ship's engines fired and it raced after the *Scimitar* while the freighter came up fast on Maul's other side. Through his viewport, Maul saw panels slide back on the freighter's hull to reveal proton-torpedo launchers.

Pirates. Maul brought his fist down on the edge of his console. He felt foolish and furious for letting down his guard, for letting his ship be sighted, for leaving himself open to an attack. He did not want any witnesses to his arrival on Tatooine. His mission was too important. But he knew that the pirates had never seen a ship like his before, that they were fully intent on seizing it. He dared not activate the *Scimitar*'s cloaking device, because that would only draw more attention to the ship's existence. The pirates would love to get their hands on an exotic cloak, and if they couldn't, they would doubtlessly talk about the ship, and their talk might reach the Jedi on Tatooine. All these thoughts raced through his head in just a few seconds.

Maul knew he would have to kill the pirates. Every one of them.

He increased energy to the *Scimitar*'s deflector shields as he angled away from the other ships, but they veered along with him and cut him off, just as he had expected. Then the space cruiser opened fire and the *Scimitar* was rocked by the blast, a warning shot. He responded by cutting power, letting his deflector shields fall. The *Scimitar* came to a dead stop in space.

Anticipating that the pirates would board the *Scimitar*, he went to the back of his ship and climbed into a cramped escape pod. As the pod's hatch sealed with a hiss, he consulted a monitor to watch the bulk freighter draw closer. An armored docking tube extended from the freighter.

Maul slid the pod's release mechanism as he activated its engine, keeping it set on low power. The pod drifted a short distance away from the *Scimitar*'s hull, and he maneuvered so the *Scimitar* concealed his position from the approaching freighter. He was not about to let anyone claim his ship. When he was certain the pirates had boarded the *Scimitar*, he guided the pod straight for the bulk freighter.

The freighter was an unremarkable model,

essentially an enormous box with a hyperdrive. Maul saw the hull was covered with grime and space dust as well as scorched by cannon fire. The freighter's docking bay was open, apparently in preparation to receive the *Scimitar.*

Maul guided his small pod into the freighter's docking bay, which was large enough to contain both the *Scimitar* and the pirate's cruiser. Illuminated by bright lamps, the docking bay was cluttered with debris and piles of rotting food. As he looked for a clear spot to land, he spotted two pirates. They were Togorians, tall beings covered with matted fur, their powerful arms ending in incredibly sharp claws. The Togorians were using their claws to tear open large metal crates, and Maul assumed the crates had been seized from some previous victim. Togorians were notoriously greedy as well as murderous.

Both Togorians glanced at the escape pod as it landed neatly in the cluttered docking bay, then returned their attention to opening the crates. Maul knew that they assumed a fellow pirate had landed the pod.

Maul opened the pod's hatch, leaped out, activated his lightsaber, and charged the two Togorians. One pirate unsheathed a vibroblade while the other snared a vibro-axe. Maul immediately evaluated that the one with the vibroblade favored his left side, and that the other pirate was clumsy. They meant nothing more to him than any other targets.

Maul flipped through the air and his blade swept

through the right side of the first pirate. The arm holding the vibroblade fell upon the deck with a sickening thud, and then the stunned Togorian collapsed beside it. Maul drove his lightsaber through the fallen pirate's chest but did not pause to watch the Togorian's body jerk and die. He was already racing toward the second pirate, who was bigger than the first.

But instead of standing his ground, the Togorian bolted away from Maul and ran for a comlink station beside a nearby hatch. Not wanting the entire ship alerted to his presence, Maul summoned the power of the dark side and focused it on the pirate. The Togorian was thrown off his feet. He flew past the comlink station and smashed into the bulkhead. Maul had intended for the impact to kill the Togorian, but the pirate, still clutching his vibro-axe, staggered back from the bulkhead and roared with rage as he turned to face his attacker.

The Togorian ran for Maul. Maul spun his lightsaber and the Togorian's wrist separated from his arm. The Togorian saw his hand and vibro-axe fall to the deck, and he howled. Maul's blade spun again, and connected with the Togorian's neck. The pirate's body collapsed.

Maul's pulse had not increased during the fight. His breathing remained steady. Deactivating his lightsaber, he stepped through a hatch and raced down a filthy corridor, littered with discarded junk, heading for the bulk freighter's bridge.

Unlike the docking bay, the bridge was dim,

primarily illuminated by sensor scopes and datascreens. Maul blinked his eyes, letting his vision adjust to the darkness, then he slunk into the bridge without a sound. Overhead, large metal cages dangled from the ceiling. The cages were filled with the motionless forms of many creatures, their faces gaping in wide-eyed agony. Maul realized the creatures had been killed but their bodies preserved, their expressions frozen at the moment of their deaths. He was disappointed that the corpses didn't include any Jedi.

Below the cages, four Togorians were staring at a console, watching a monitor that displayed another Togorian, who was standing within the *Scimitar*. The on-screen Togorian's fur was elaborately braided and ornamented with glittering objects. Over the comlink, the pirate with the boarding party reported, "I'm telling you, there's no one on board!"

One of the four Togorians who stood before the monitor wore a necklace made from assorted skulls. Maul guessed him to be the captain and knew he was correct by the way the Togorian barked, "You looked for hidden compartments?"

Sounding exasperated, the Togorian on the monitor replied, "Of course we searched for hidden compartments, we're not fools! It's an unmanned ship. The course was set for Tatooine. That's why it didn't answer the distress signal. Have you ever seen a ship like this? I haven't!"

The captain appeared to be weighing his options, then growled, "All right, idiot. Bring both ships into the loading dock. The bay is still open. If you do find any passengers, kill them."

The captain broke the connection and the monitor went dark. One of the other pirates growled, "Hela-Tan is a fool. They could be in hiding."

"Then we'll find them," the second pirate said.

"Or they could have escaped," added the third.

"Shut your flapping mouth," snorted the Togorian captain. "What's the difference? We have the ship." He turned away from the others.

Maul moved fast. He activated his lightsaber and cut the nearest Togorian in half. The Togorian did not cry out, but the noise of his collapsing body caused his fellow pirates to turn. The captain faced Maul, baring his fangs. Drawing two vibro-axes from his belt, the captain roared, "Prepare to die, scum!"

Maul wondered why so many opponents felt compelled to announce their intentions with threats and taunts. Deciding to save the captain for last, he flipped across the bridge, kicked the second pirate in the throat, and then drove his lightsaber through the pirate's chest. The second pirate fell.

The third pirate whipped out a vibroblade. Maul charged him. As Maul's lightsaber cleaved through his target, he sensed that the captain was taking aim at his back. Leaping from the third pirate's dead body,

Maul soared backward over the captain's head just as the captain's vibro-axes met with a loud, energized shriek where Maul had been standing just a fraction of a second earlier. Maul grabbed hold of the bars on an overhead cage and swung himself to land behind the captain.

The clashing vibro-axes ignited, illuminating the remains of the caged wretches and casting ghastly shadows throughout the bridge. Prying his vibro-axes away from each other, the captain turned to face Maul again. Blood pounded in Maul's ears as he spun his lightsaber, slashing the captain's arms before delivering a killing blow.

From the comm console, a Togorian's voice crackled, "Approaching docking bay."

Maul stepped to the console. He did not activate the visual monitor as he lowered his face over the comm and said, "Proceed to the bridge." Then Maul turned his attention to the freighter's computer. He knew Togorian pirates always fled the scene of a crime immediately to avoid capture. And thanks to his mechanical training with Sidious, it took only a few seconds to interface the freighter's propulsion units with the proton torpedoes. The moment the Togorians punched the ignition for their engines, the entire ship would blow up.

Leaving the bridge, Maul ran back to the docking bay. He heard the pirates approaching and ducked into a side corridor. He watched the pirates stagger past his position, heading toward the bridge. They were already arguing about how they should divide the spoils from the strange, newly acquired starship.

After the Togorians were gone, Maul hurried across the brightly lit bay. The *Scimitar* rested beside the pirates' space cruiser. He ran past the escape pod that had delivered him to the docking bay. He had already resolved that he did not have time to recover the pod.

The *Scimitar*'s boarding ramp was down. Maul ran up the ramp and nearly collided with the Togorian whose fur was decorated with glittering objects. Up close, Maul saw that the objects were sharp razors, and that this Togorian was bigger than the others. Much bigger.

Maul surmised the pirate had remained on the ship so he could take what he wanted before the others had their chance. The pirate was holding two fistfuls of credits that Maul kept aboard for emergencies, and was about to deposit the credits in an open satchel at his feet. Maul saw the satchel was bulging, and suspected the pirate had also found his stash of crystals, which he kept for worlds that did not accept credits.

Maul activated his lightsaber. The pirate tossed the credits aside and removed his vibro-axe from his belt. Eyes fixed on Maul, the pirate said, "There you are." He stuck out his thick purple tongue and dragged it across his lips. "Think you can escape me? Think again. I'll finish the job."

Maul was irritated by the Togorians' tendency to taunt before striking. He was also eager to leave the freighter, as he expected the other pirates would start the engines at any moment. He whirled in an arc and went for the hulking Togorian's chest.

Incredibly, the pirate sidestepped the attack. His vibro-axe swept past Maul's shoulder but smashed into the *Scimitar*'s auxiliary control console. Maul saw the damage was minimal, but seethed with rage. Hoping to prevent further damage to his ship, he leaped past the pirate and flipped down the *Scimitar*'s boarding ramp. The pirate followed.

Jumping to the docking bay's deck, the pirate shook his fur, and his glittering, decorative shards reflected the lights from the bright lamps that illuminated the docking bay. The light momentarily dazzled Maul's vision, causing him to lose focus as the pirate swung his vibro-axe. Maul jumped away, but not before the vibro-axe's blade caught his leg. Maul felt the blade slice into his flesh. He bared his teeth as if he were biting on the pain itself.

He glared at his opponent, then leaped and twisted in midair, spinning his lightsaber at the pirate. Maul's blade took off the pirate's arm before landing. The pirate collapsed, and Maul struck him again, but it was not a killing blow because he did not wish for the pirate to die immediately. He wanted the pirate to die in agony.

Ignoring his own wound, Maul deactivated his lightsaber, jumped over the pirate's body, and raced back up the *Scimitar*'s boarding ramp. Although he wished he were already seated behind the controls on the upper deck, he didn't dare waste the few seconds it would take for the lift to carry him to the bridge. As the boarding ramp automatically retracted, he went straight to the auxiliary control console that the Togorian had struck earlier. He was checking the console to make sure it was fully operational when he heard a loud hum outside his ship. He knew the noise was the freighter's preliminary ignition warming up. He tapped at the console's controls and powered up the *Scimitar*'s shields and engines.

A warning light flashed. The *Scimitar*'s ramp had retracted but the hatch was still open. Maul heard an inhuman roar from behind and turned to see that the hulking pirate—minus one arm, and with his face covered in blood—had wedged himself into the boarding hatch, his body pinned between the hatch's doors. Clutching to the inner hatch with his remaining hand's bloodied claws, the Togorian wasn't about to let go on his own.

The pirate's legs were still dangling out of the hatch as Maul pushed the *Scimitar*'s engines to full power and blasted out of the freighter's docking bay. Alarms wailed as air rushed out the open hatch. As the *Scimitar* soared into space, Maul was yanked off his feet and hurled toward the pirate in the hatch.

Maul's wounded leg slammed against the bulkhead inside the hatch. Air was torn from his lungs as his fingers seized a metal rung. His face was mere centimeters from the Togorian's, and he could see from the pirate's frenzied expression that he had every intention of making sure Maul died with him.

Maul rammed his horned head into the pirate's skull. The pirate's one-handed grip loosened. Maul twisted his body and kicked the pirate's midsection. The pirate roared and sank his claws into the inside of the hatch's frame. The dark side surged through Maul, and he kicked the pirate in the face.

Behind the *Scimitar*, the bulk freighter exploded, spraying burning fuel and shredded metal in all directions. The resulting shock wave rocked the *Scimitar*, and the Togorian was blown away from the hatch. Maul hit the hatch's emergency button and it sealed instantly, sending him rolling back into the *Scimitar*.

Emergency air flooded into the lower deck. Maul gasped as he scrambled onto the lift. Arriving on the upper deck, he did not limp as he went to his seat and settled behind the controls. He took a deep breath. He felt good to be alive after his enemies were dead.

Angling away from the wreckage of the pirate ships, he guided the *Scimitar* toward Tatooine. He knew he should treat his wound soon but decided to wait until after he'd landed. Meanwhile, his pain gave him something to focus on.

He was looking forward to finding more enemies.

From space, Tatooine looked like a scorched sphere with just a few small, scattered clouds. The *Scimitar*'s sensors directed Maul to the planet's larger spaceports and settlements, and he was pleased to see that night had fallen over those areas. From experience, he had come to prefer night landings, because most so-called civilized beings liked to have their lights on at night. They revealed themselves. Even Sand People and Jawas were known to huddle around open fires after the twin suns set.

As the *Scimitar* descended to the sand planet's dark hemisphere, Maul began to see the lights of the more populated areas as well as solitary moisture farms. Queen Amidala's ship could be anywhere on Tatooine, but he was confident he would find it.

He landed his ship on a mesa. He did not leave the *Scimitar* until he was certain that no detectors were aimed in his direction and that he had arrived unnoticed. Carrying his electrobinoculars, and wearing a programmable wrist link above his left hand, he stepped down the boarding ramp and onto the hard-packed sand. The air was cool and incredibly dry, and a few stars were already visible in the evening sky.

Maul came to a stop. From where he stood, he could see the distant lights of three settlements. His electrobinoculars were equipped with radiation sensors for night vision and powerful light-gathering components for long-distance scanning. He raised the electrobinoculars to his eyes and scanned the terrain to his left. According to the data display on his electrobinocular viewscreen, he was looking at Mos Espa, one of Tatooine's largest spaceports.

Turning almost completely around, Maul viewed the city of Mos Taike, which was located between the Northern Dune Sea and another broad area of barren desert, the Xelric Draw. Shifting to his left, he viewed another spaceport, Mos Entha.

Maul lowered the electrobinoculars, tapped a command into his wrist link to summon his probe droids, and turned to face the *Scimitar*. He watched three bulbous, black Dark Eye probe droids hover out of the aft hatch. Each sensor-laden probe droid had been programmed to seek out Queen Amidala, her ship, and the two Jedi who had escaped with her from Naboo.

The three probe droids glided past Maul before they separated, each veering off toward one of the three populated areas. After they were gone, Maul trudged back to the *Scimitar* so he could monitor the droids' progress. The sand sucked at his boots, making every step an effort.

Sweat beaded on his tattooed forehead. His wounded leg was practically screaming for treatment. But even after he was back inside the *Scimitar*, he delayed reaching for a medpac. He worked with the pain, manipulating it, shaping it into desire. He craved revenge against the Jedi. They were the reason he had traveled to Tatooine. If not for their existence, his encounter with the Togorian pirates never would have happened. His desire for vengeance grew like a blanket of darkness around him. Only after he felt consumed by anger did he dress his wound.

Maul grinned. The pain was nothing compared to what he would do to the Jedi.

CHAPTER FIFTEEN

Maul unloaded his speeder bike from the *Scimitar*'s underside cargo hatch. It was the day after his arrival on Tatooine, and the twin suns were blazing in the sky. He had already received significant transmissions from his three probe droids.

The first probe droid had sighted a tall, bearded man carrying a lightsaber at Mos Espa Grand Arena after a Podracing competition. The second probe droid had been destroyed—possibly by a lightsaber—before it transmitted an image of a run-down light freighter named the *Dusty Duck*, which had simply been in the wrong place at the wrong time. Fortunately, the third probe droid had discovered the location of Queen Amidala's starship in the Xelric Draw. Now Maul was waiting for the first probe droid to return with a full report from Mos Espa. And he wanted his bike ready if he needed it.

The bike was a custom Razalon FC-20 repulsorlift speeder, equipped with a quiet but powerful rear thrust engine, ideal for covert missions and sneak attacks. The bike had no built-in weapons, sensors, or shields, as Maul believed his own skills and lightsaber were sufficient to overcome any enemy.

Thanks to the combination of his discipline and remarkable powers of recuperation, Maul did not limp as he walked, using one hand to nudge his bike through the arid air, away from his ship. He had treated his leg with bacta and wrapped it in bandages. When he was fully healed, not even a scar would exist as evidence of his fight with the Togorian.

But his leg still ached. Earlier, after discovering bantha tracks near the *Scimitar*, he had had a brief encounter with Sand People. He suspected they had intended to lure him away from his ship and kill him. He had refrained from slaughtering them because a pile of dead Sand People might have drawn unnecessary attention. Still, running back to the *Scimitar* had not been good for his leg.

I'll rest after the Jedi are dead.

Maul left his bike hovering in the air behind him and came to a stop at the edge of the mesa. He gazed toward Mos Espa. And then he saw the probe droid zipping over the sand, approaching his position. The probe droid came to a stop less than a meter away from Maul's face. The droid uttered a few words in its own language, but Maul understood.

A Jedi had left Mos Espa and was returning to the Queen's ship.

Maul walked back to his bike, climbed onto its saddle, and launched off the mesa, leaving the watchful probe droid with the *Scimitar*. Maul's black cloak whipped at his back as he raced over the desert floor and into the Xelric Draw.

He soon saw the Queen's starship, still resting where his droid had sighted it earlier. Despite a layer of dust, the ship's highly polished silver exterior gleamed under the bright desert sky. The ship's boarding ramp was lowered.

And then Maul sighted two figures in front of him, both running toward the ship. The nearest figure appeared to be a child, a young boy. Beyond the boy was the tall Jedi.

Maul sensed something about the boy. The boy seemed to emanate ripples in the Force, but the ripples were unfocused, uncontrolled. This surprised Maul but did not distract him. He stayed focused on his target, the Jedi. If he happened also to mow down the boy in his path, so be it.

Maul accelerated. He was almost on top of the boy when the Jedi turned and shouted, and then the boy fell flat to the ground. As Maul's bike passed over the boy's prone body, Maul realized the Jedi must have commanded the boy to fall. He was intrigued by the fact that the boy had obeyed without hesitation, without looking back. Most boys would have stopped and turned.

Dismissing the boy as insignificant, Maul cut the bike's engine and leaped from it, sailing over the Jedi's head as he activated his lightsaber in midair. The Jedi activated his own green-bladed lightsaber and raised it fast to block Maul's sweeping blade. The lightsabers met with a bright flash of energy before Maul landed on his feet in a tight crouch.

The pain in his leg was exquisite.

Up close, Maul saw the Jedi was a big man. The Jedi shouted at the boy to go. Maul swung hard with his lightsaber but the Jedi blocked the blow. The Jedi shouted, "Tell them to take off!"

As the boy ran for the Queen's ship, Maul lashed out at the Jedi again and again, but the Jedi blocked each blow. Maul was suddenly aware that the Jedi seemed to anticipate each lunge and jab, as if he knew how Maul would move before Maul himself knew. Maul drew from the dark side of the Force and began to move faster, increasing the speed of his lunges along with his footwork. The Jedi kept up with Maul, but Maul soon sensed . . .

He's getting tired.

Maul felt the pain in his leg become more intense. He became angry at himself for being wounded, used the anger to fuel the dark side, and directed his rage at the Jedi. Maul was certain he would defeat his opponent.

He will fall heavily, like a monument.

But the Jedi did not falter. As Maul spun and moved around the Jedi, he saw the Queen's starship lift off. He also saw the boarding ramp was still extended.

Maul leaped over the Jedi, blocking his path to the rising ship, as their lightsabers continued to weave and smash into each other. The ship had just moved above their position when the Jedi leaped straight up and landed on the extended ramp, his lightsaber still blazing.

Maul watched the ship rise away from the desert, taking the Jedi with it. He deactivated his lightsaber and continued to stand where his feet were planted. Within seconds, the ascending ship vanished in the sky.

Maul tasted sand in his mouth. And blood. He continued to watch the sky as he felt almost overwhelmed by his humiliation. He had never felt such shame before. The shame was darker than any darkness he had ever known.

He found the darkness pleasing.

Maul had no reason to remain on Tatooine. He recovered his speeder bike and rode back to the *Scimitar*.

He transmitted a report, notifying his Master that the Jedi had escaped with Queen Amidala, and that he would be returning directly to Coruscant. He did not mention his run-in with the Togorian pirates in his report, nor his less significant encounter with the Sand People, because he knew his Master would be displeased. His Master would not be interested in explanations. His Master would only accuse him of allowing himself to be snared by the pirates and distracted by the Sand People.

As the Sith Infiltrator lifted away from Tatooine, Maul continued to contemplate how Sidious would respond if he learned about his apprentice's mis-adventures. If Maul admitted he had sustained a leg wound, his Master would regard him as weak. But because his leg wound was already almost healed, he questioned whether it was even necessary to inform his Master about it.

Concealing details from his Master was impossible. Sidious always knew everything about Maul's thoughts and actions. However, Maul knew his Master would not wish to be distracted by information that had nothing to do with conquering Naboo and destroying the Jedi. A wounded leg was beyond trivial. If he and his Master were to proceed, they would focus on moving forward.

The Sith Infiltrator left Tatooine's orbit and launched into hyperspace.

CHAPTER SIXTEEN

Droid Attak

Arriving at Coruscant, Maul guided the *Scimitar* to the dark hemisphere, where night had fallen, angling past illuminated skyscrapers to the spire that housed Sidious's secret headquarters. He docked the Infiltrator in a landing bay, checked to make sure the landing bay was secure, and then went to meet with his Master.

He found Sidious's hooded figure seated in the middle of the otherwise empty meditation room. The door slid closed behind Maul. Sidious said, "Report."

"Queen Amidala and the Jedi *were* on Tatooine, Master. A Jedi and a young boy were running for the Queen's starship when I came upon them in the desert. The Jedi and I dueled. I nearly had him. But the boy reached the ship, the ship lifted off, and the Jedi leaped to it. I failed to stop them, Master."

Because of his Master's cowl, Maul could not see his

Master's eyes, but he watched the lower half of Sidious's face, staying alert for any slight twitch at the mouth or change in skin tone that would indicate his Master was angry. But his Master's expression remained neutral as he said, "You feel you would have defeated this Jedi?"

"Yes, Master. I felt him tire. I can defeat him."

"Was he bearded?"

Maul nodded.

"Good. That is Qui-Gon Jinn. He is the stronger of the two. His Padawan is Obi-Wan Kenobi."

Sidious sounded satisfied, which puzzled Maul. He had imagined Sidious would be furious with him for failing to stop the Jedi and the Queen. But then it suddenly occurred to Maul . . . *The Jedi will deliver the Queen to Coruscant, because the foolish Queen will think the Senate can help her.* Maul realized he could have another opportunity to please his Master. But before he could announce his deduction, his Master said, "Queen Amidala believes the Galactic Senate will support her. She has already arrived on Coruscant. She is staying in the Senatorial quarters."

Maul stiffened. "And the Jedi?"

"They are on Coruscant as well."

Maul's hand shifted to the hilt of his lightsaber. He felt a burning that began in his chest and spread outward. "Let me kill them, Master."

"Not here," Sidious said. "Not on Coruscant. I have another plan."

And then Maul sensed Sidious was preoccupied by other thoughts. He seemed oblivious to Maul's presence. Maul left the meditation room and went to his own quarters.

As soon as he was alone, he wondered whether his Master was actually furious and was now only delaying punishment. *Is he aware of my battle with the pirates? Of my foolish decision to follow the bantha tracks? Did he sense my leg wound?* Maul would not be surprised if his Master was just waiting to punish him like never before. He felt ashamed.

But then he thought of his Master's teachings. *Think of the now. Think of the future. Do not meditate on the past.*

Maul knew what he must do. He would use his shame, turn it inward to feed the darkness and hatred that flowed through his veins. He would direct his fury at his enemy, the Jedi named Qui-Gon Jinn.

In the past, Maul had never cared about the names of the people he'd killed. To him, enemies were nothing more than targets. But now he said Qui-Gon Jinn's name aloud. He clenched his teeth and repeated the name, then began chanting it like a curse.

I will destroy you, Qui-Gon Jinn. I will see the shock in your eyes when I run you through, Qui-Gon Jinn.

I will stand over your dead body in triumph, Qui-Gon Jinn.

Because of you, I have failed my Master.
You will pay.

Hours passed. Maul's comlink chirped. His Master was summoning him to the strategy room. Maul went. He found his Master shrugging out of the robe he wore in his guise as Palpatine, and realized his Master had returned from the Senate building.

"Queen Amidala will attempt to bring the Senate to her cause," Sidious said with pleasure. "She will ask them to outlaw the Trade Federation blockade of Naboo." He chortled happily.

Maul had never seen his Master in such a jovial mood. He thought, *My mistakes don't matter. Unless he is distracted by current events and will turn on me later . . .*

"I anticipate the Queen will return to Naboo," Sidious continued. "No doubt the Jedi will accompany her. Foolish girl." He smiled at Maul. "Come. Let us contact the Neimoidians and share the good news."

Sidious pulled on his dark robe, lifted its hood up over his head, stood before the communications console, and activated the holocomm. Maul stayed out of sight in the alcove behind Sidious's seat and watched as holograms of Nute Gunray and Rune Haako materialized in the air. Many light-years away, in Theed Royal Palace on the planet Naboo, Nute looked anxious as he said, "Yes, Lord Sidious?"

"The Queen will soon be on her way to you. I regret she is of no further use to us. Destroy her when she arrives."

Nute nodded. "Yes, my lord."

"Is the planet secure?"

"We have taken over the last pockets of primitive life-forms. We are in complete control of the planet now."

"Good," Sidious said. "I will see to it that in the Senate, things stay as they are. I am sending my apprentice, Darth Maul, to join you."

"Yes, my lord."

Sidious broke the connection and the holograms disappeared. Still facing the comm console, he laughed. "Soon the Neimoidians will no longer be useful to us. What a fine day that will be." He turned to face Maul. "Make sure the Neimoidians take care of Queen Amidala. You yourself must destroy the Jedi. Do not fail me again."

Maul bowed to his Master, then left quickly for the Sith Infiltrator.

When the *Scimitar* exited hyperspace in the Naboo system, Maul saw a single Droid Control Ship, the only remnant of the Trade Federation's blockade, in Naboo's orbit. Although the Neimoidians were expecting his arrival, Maul had activated the *Scimitar*'s cloaking technology to guarantee they would not be aware of his ship approaching the planet. He thought it would be best if he presented himself to Nute Gunray unannounced.

Naboo was a small world, covered by grassy plains, verdant mountains, and clear, unpolluted seas and lakes. As Maul descended through the atmosphere, he saw a flock of large, graceful birds soaring away from a waterfall that plunged over the edge of a steep cliff. Maul imagined what Naboo would be like if it were reduced to a lifeless, smoldering rock. He grinned at the thought.

He guided the *Scimitar* to the capital city of Theed. The city's architecture consisted primarily of elegantly designed domed structures, most of which appeared quite old but also well maintained. The largest structure was Theed Royal Palace, an interconnected cluster of domed spires that rose from a high cliff. As Maul landed his ship, he thought of Queen Amidala growing up in such rich, comfortable surroundings, with her handmaidens and assorted servants seeing to her every need.

Pampered weaklings.

From Maul's perspective, death could not come soon enough for the people of Naboo.

The Neimoidians had seized Theed Royal Palace as their own headquarters, and had settled into its lavish rooms as if they had owned it for years. Maul found Nute Gunray in Queen Amidala's private bedroom. He was lying sound asleep on a plush couch, a coverlet of soft shimmersilk draped over his body. Maul yanked away the coverlet and delivered a swift, hard kick to Nute's side.

Waking in a panic, Nute exclaimed, "Are they invading?!" And then he saw Darth Maul looming over him.

Maul glared with open disgust at the Neimoidian leader. "Get out. These are now my quarters."

Nute scrambled to his feet. He was taller than Maul, but Maul looked at him as if he were an insignificant bug. Nute tried to take the shimmersilk coverlet with him, but Maul snatched it and tore it in half. Maul said, "Send someone to remove the traces of your presence here."

Eager to distance himself from Maul, Nute shuffled quickly out of the bedroom. Maul looked around at the Queen's furnishings and laughed. He had no desire to sleep in such an extravagant room, but he had enjoyed terrifying Nute.

Leaving the bedroom, Maul thoroughly inspected the palace. Everywhere he looked, from the floor-to-ceiling windows to the grand hallways and staircases, he saw evidence of fine craftsmanship. He reconsidered the bedroom. Although he had been raised to associate luxury with weakness, he found satisfaction in the idea that there was nothing to stop him from claiming the palace as his own. There were no rules for how and where the Sith Lords should live *after* they achieved their goals, and Maul doubted that his Master expected him to rule from a small room with bare walls. He wondered if he had been too quick to envision laying waste to the entire planet. He could imagine worse fates than ruling from the opulent palace. And the Naboo plains and forests were rich with wild beasts ready for slaughter.

He made his way to the throne room. There he found Nute, seated on the throne, talking with Rune Haako. The Neimoidians looked up with alarm as Maul approached. Maul took pleasure in watching Nute cling desperately to the throne's broad arms, as if Maul might yank it out from underneath him. Maul said, "Status report."

Unable to meet Maul's gaze, Nute blinked his large eyes and said, "Things are . . . er, going well."

"Most of the Naboo people have been captured," Rune chimed in. "We have them in camps. A few have eluded us, but we shall crush them soon. As for Queen Amidala, every Trade Federation troop in the area is on alert, watching for her ship. We expect her to land in the city's central plaza, and that she will attempt to negotiate with us while using the Jedi as her shields. She will not slip through any of our safeguards."

Maul scowled. "Unless she is already here."

The Neimoidians glanced at each other and cried out at the same time, "Impossible!"

"I suggest we inspect the security around the plaza."

Nute and Rune babbled their approval. They shuffled

after Maul as he led them outside to the wide plaza. Maul imagined that the plaza was usually crowded with citizens, musicians, and merchants and the air was filled with conversation and singing birds. But now the only sound was the distant, clanking footfalls of droid troops. Maul enjoyed the desolation. However, he was not deceived by the overall quiet. Looking up at the cloudless sky, he thought, *A storm is coming. A death storm.*

Jedi will die.

Rune pointed to a detachment of Federation battle droids that was marching across the opposite end of the plaza. He said, "They are timed to cover the plaza every fifteen minutes."

"Make it every five," Maul said as he scanned the surrounding buildings.

"But Lord Maul," Rune said uneasily, "what of the few citizens who have so far resisted us? Shouldn't we keep the troops spread out?"

Maul fixed his yellow eyes on Rune. "Do you think," Maul said, "the Queen will dawdle when she arrives, and simply wait for you to pick her up? *Think*, cretin. Where do you think she'll be heading?"

"Five-minute patrols!" Nute barked into his comlink. "Cover the plaza every five minutes!"

Maul gestured to the balconies that overlooked the plaza. "There should be surveillance at all times. Infrared sensors to alert the patrols."

"It shall be done," Rune said.

Nute's comlink signaled. He glanced at it anxiously.

"I suggest you answer that," Maul said, "or I'll throw you over a waterfall."

Nute pressed a button on his comlink and said, "Report."

The voice of a battle droid command officer responded flatly, "The Queen's starship has been found in the Naboo swamps, Viceroy."

Nute looked stunned. "Have you captured her?"

"The ship is empty, Viceroy," the officer replied. "There is no sign of the Queen's party. They have disappeared."

Nute and Rune glanced at each other. Rune's mouth was agape. Neither dared to face Maul. Still clutching the comlink, Nute said, voice trembling, "Send out patrols. Search for her."

Maul grabbed the comlink and switched it off. Through clenched teeth, he hissed at Nute, "Everything is under control, you say? You'll pay for this. Now we must contact Lord Sidious."

Nute nodded obediently as his mottled face turned a more sickly shade of green.

Maul led the two Neimoidians back to the palace's throne room. Nute seated himself quickly on the throne. Maul stood near Nute while Rune activated the holo-comm, sending a transmission to Sidious. A moment later, a hologram of Maul's hooded Master flickered to life. Sidious said, "Yes, Viceroy?"

"Lord Sidious." Nute cleared his throat. "The Queen and the Jedi . . . they are on Naboo, but did not arrive where we expected."

Sidious frowned slightly, then said, "Go on."

"We've sent out patrols," Nute continued. "We already located their starship in the swamp. It won't be long, my lord."

"This is an unexpected move for her," Sidious said. "It's too aggressive." His hologram shifted. Even though Sidious's eyes were lost in shadow, Maul knew that his Master's gaze was now on him. "Lord Maul, be mindful. Let them make the first move."

"Yes, my Master."

While the Neimoidians scurried about the palace, Maul stood in a dark chamber near the throne room and meditated. He visualized the fight he knew would come, the inevitable duel with Qui-Gon Jinn. On Tatooine, he knew he had been wearing down the Jedi Knight. He had sensed that Qui-Gon Jinn fought without fear, but also without hate.

He will know fear. And I will make him hate me.

Maul heard someone running toward him. Annoyed by the interruption, he turned to face Nute Gunray. Nute cried out, "She is assembling an army!"

CHAPTER SEVENTEEN

"According to our patrols," Rune Haako said, "Queen Amidala contacted the Gungans, the primitives in the swamp."

Maul had not anticipated that the Queen would join forces with the Gungans, Naboo's amphibious natives. He turned to face Nute Gunray. "You said the primitives had all been rounded up."

"They went into hiding!" Nute exclaimed. "They know the terrain better than we do. . . ." Seeing Maul's angered glare, Nute went silent.

Rune said, "The Gungans are not a concern. They are no match for our forces. The Trade Federation droid army and weapons are invincible."

Maul could only guess what Queen Amidala thought she might accomplish. All her starfighters had been confiscated. Her volunteer pilots and officers were being held in camps. Desperate for help, she had turned to her planet's lesser life-forms, amphibious humanoids. Still, she had the Jedi on her side. Unable to determine what the Queen was planning, Maul said, "I must contact my Master."

"We should return to the throne room," Rune Haako said, gesturing to a four-legged Neimoidian mechno-holoprojector he had brought for Nute Gunray's convenience.

"We'll walk," Maul said as he went to the holoprojector and activated it. Less than a minute later, Sidious's hologram appeared, his gaze directed at Maul, Nute, and Rune, who followed the ambulatory device as it crawled through a palace corridor on its sharply tapered metal feet.

"The Queen has an army, my Master," Maul said. "She has allied with Naboo's Gungan population. They must be planning to strike against the Trade Federation's superior forces." Maul grimaced. "I feel there is more to this, my Master. The two Jedi may be using the Queen for their own purposes."

"The Jedi cannot become involved," Sidious said with authority, his hologram bobbing gently back and forth along with the movement of the walking holo-projector. "They can only protect the Queen. Even Qui-Gon Jinn will not break that covenant."

Maul had not considered the fact that the Jedi, by tradition and the rules of their Order, did not fight in wars. His Master never overlooked any details.

"Our young Queen surprises me," Sidious continued. "She is more foolish than I thought."

Nute said, "We are sending all troops to meet this army assembling near the swamp. It appears to be made up of primitives."

"This will work to our advantage," Sidious responded. Maul noticed that his Master actually sounded pleased.

The holoprojector came to a stop in the corridor. Maul, Nute, and Rune stopped beside it, their eyes fixed on Sidious's hologram. Rune said eagerly, "I have your approval to proceed, then, my lord?"

"Wipe them out," Sidious replied without hesitation. "All of them." Sidious's hologram flickered and vanished.

Maul, Nute, and Rune proceeded to the throne room. A large viewscreen was built into one wall, and displayed a view of the palace's outdoor plaza. Looking up at the viewscreen, the Neimoidians were startled to see the Jedi Knight and his apprentice cutting down battle droids who had been guarding the palace. The Jedi were accompanied by Naboo soldiers and pilots. Some soldiers were on foot, and others arrived in armored landspeeders that carried blaster cannons.

Rune whispered, "How did they get into the city?"

"I don't know," Nute said, shaking his head as he watched the Naboo soldiers fire Federation tanks. "I thought the battle was going to take place far from here." Eyes wide with fear, he added, "This is too close."

"I told you there was more to this," Maul said. "The Jedi *are* involved. They have come to Theed for a reason, Viceroy. They have a plan of their own for defeating us."

Looking even more alarmed, Nute said, "A plan?"

"One that will fail, I assure you." Maul glared at the images on the viewscreen. "I have waited a long time for this. I have trained for it endlessly. The Jedi will regret their decision to return here." His hand flexed near his lightsaber. "Wait here until I return." He walked past the Neimoidians, heading for a tall doorway.

"Where are you going?" Nute demanded frantically.

"Where do you think I'm going, Viceroy?" Maul answered without breaking his stride. "I'm going to the main hangar to rid you of the Jedi once and for all."

The Queen's pilots managed to liberate more than a dozen Naboo starfighters from the Theed hangar before Maul's arrival. Maul saw the sleek, gleaming starfighters climb into the sky and suspected they were heading for the Trade Federation's Droid Control Ship. Because the control ship carried more than one thousand droid starfighters, Maul doubted the Queen's pilots would survive more than a few minutes. *Fools.*

He entered the air base and made his way to the hangar's entrance, which was sealed by blast-proof durasteel double doors. Lowering his gaze to the floor, he reached out with his senses. He detected movement on the other side of the doors. He knew the Jedi were approaching, walking straight toward his position.

The double doors slid open. Maul lifted his gaze. He faced Queen Amidala, who was with a group of armed Naboo guards and two handmaidens. Seeing Maul, the group had come to a dead stop. Maul spotted the two Jedi behind the guards and locked his eyes on Qui-Gon Jinn.

"We'll handle this," Qui-Gon Jinn said as he and Obi-Wan Kenobi moved forward, side by side, edging past the guards.

"We'll take the long way," Queen Amidala said as she rushed with her remaining allies toward a side passage.

Keeping his eyes on the Jedi, Maul lifted his hood back, revealing his horned head. He shrugged off his cloak and let it fall to the floor. The two Jedi did the same with their robes.

The Queen, her guards, and the handmaidens were still running for a nearby exit when three Trade Federation destroyer droids wheeled fast from around a corner and into the hangar. The droids stopped quickly, then rapidly unfurled their tripod legs and built-in blaster cannons, activated their deflector shields, and opened fire in the Queen's direction.

While the Queen and her retinue took cover and fired their blasters at the droids, Maul drew his lightsaber and activated one red blade. Gripping the lightsaber in his left hand, he extended his arm forward and activated the second blade. The Jedi activated their lightsabers, and Maul noticed Qui-Gon Jinn's blade flashed a fraction of a second after Obi-Wan's.

The old Jedi's getting slow.

Maul made a jabbing motion at Obi-Wan. Obi-Wan leaped at Maul. Their lightsabers clashed as Obi-Wan flipped over Maul's head and landed behind him. Keeping his eyes on Qui-Gon, Maul angled his lightsaber to block Obi-Wan's blade from behind, then ducked fast to evade Qui-Gon's sweeping blade.

Maul advanced toward Qui-Gon and spun, deflecting blows from both Jedi as the fight shifted across the hangar deck. Rapidly spinning his lightsaber, he anticipated their moves with ease. Having expected a greater challenge from Qui-Gon and Obi-Wan, he felt even more disgusted by them. But if the Jedi held no surprises in combat, Maul knew he had his Master to thank for that. If not for his Master, he never would have been a match for two Jedi at the same time.

Over the crashing noise of lightsabers, the destroyer droids' cannons, and the Naboo guards' blasters, Maul heard a starfighter's laser cannon firing across the hangar. He did not need the Force to be peripherally aware that the shots came from one remaining Naboo starfighter, which had just lifted off the deck and was now angling for the destroyer droids. He kept up his assault on the Jedi while the starfighter fired again and again, knocking out the destroyer droids' shields before shattering them completely. A moment later, the Queen and her group fled through a doorway, and then the Naboo starfighter soared out of the hangar.

Maul was not worried about the Queen. He would deal with her later. But for the moment, he was busy.

He kicked Qui-Gon in the chest so hard that he knocked the Jedi off his feet. He flipped away from Obi-Wan, flinging his body through the air to land before a doorway that led to Theed City's power generator. With one hand gripping his lightsaber, he reached out with the Force and seized a large piece of debris from one of the ruined destroyer droids, then launched it at the door's opening mechanism. The mechanism exploded in sparks and the door began to slide open.

Qui-Gon was already up and he rushed toward Maul, but Obi-Wan reached him first. Maul spun his lightsaber, deflecting his opponents' strikes as he backed through the open doorway. He launched a high kick that connected with Obi-Wan's jaw. As Obi-Wan fell back and rolled across the floor, Maul backed up, luring Qui-Gon toward the power generator. Obi-Wan got up fast and sprinted to rejoin the fight.

That's it. Come to me.

Qui-Gon swung. Maul parried and swung back fast, clipping Qui-Gon's blade and then Obi-Wan's. The

197

double-bladed lightsaber was a blur. Maul backed onto an inspection platform that was suspended high over the generator's deep shaft, and kicked off, backflipping to one of the many catwalks that spanned different levels in the shaft. Both Jedi leaped after him, and the fight proceeded along the catwalk.

Maul leered at the Jedi as he edged around a towering acceleration shaft that glowed brightly with plasma used to energize Theed City. With his lightsaber in constant motion, he kicked Obi-Wan straight off the catwalk. Before he could determine whether Obi-Wan had plummeted to his death, Qui-Gon struck and surprised Maul with a backhanded blow to the head that sent Maul over the catwalk's edge.

Maul did not cry out. He knew the shaft's central catwalk lay below him. He kept his lightsaber activated and held its pommel close to his chest as he landed hard on his back on the catwalk. The impact would have broken an ordinary man's back, but Maul was not by any means ordinary. He did feel pain, but as ever, the pain only fueled his rage.

He was still lying on his back as he saw Qui-Gon leaping from above. The Jedi landed close to him, and Maul had to move fast to block the Jedi's blade. Then Maul was up again, moving backward along the central catwalk. In the distance, beyond Qui-Gon's back, Maul sighted Obi-Wan clinging to the edge of a lower catwalk. Maul realized he didn't want Obi-Wan to fall, because that would deprive him of the pleasure of killing the young Jedi.

Maul leered again at Qui-Gon. *You think you're driving me back. You have no idea that I'm in control. You don't know where I'm taking you.*

The central catwalk terminated at the entrance of a security hallway that led to the generator's core. The hallway was protected by six consecutive laser doors that opened and locked shut in response to potentially lethal power outputs that occurred intermittently during the generator's plasma-activation process. As Maul lured Qui-Gon toward the hallway, he saw Obi-Wan leap up onto the central catwalk.

You'll both be dead soon.

Maul sensed the laser doors opening behind him. Qui-Gon was unrelenting in his ongoing attack, but Maul parried every blow. Qui-Gon swung at Maul's legs, but the blade swept under his feet as Maul jumped backward. Maul continued moving back, leading Qui-Gon into the hallway. They passed the first four security barriers before the doors activated and shut.

Transparent red curtains of pure energy, the doors would kill any life-form on contact. Maul was suddenly sealed in the passage between the fifth and sixth doors, and Qui-Gon between the fourth and fifth. Gazing past Qui-Gon, Maul saw Obi-Wan trapped between the first and second doors.

Facing Maul, Qui-Gon deactivated his lightsaber and dropped to one knee. Maul jabbed at the laser door that separated him from the Jedi, and succeeded only in producing a noisy flash. Maul deactivated his own weapon and watched the Jedi warily. He watched Qui-Gon take a deep breath and close his eyes.

He's . . . meditating?!

Keeping his eyes on the kneeling Jedi, Maul paced back and forth within his confined area of the hallway. He was baffled by the Jedi's mentality, the urge to meditate at such a moment, the desire to remain calm. The effort was so pointless. Glancing through the doors behind Qui-Gon, Maul saw that the worried-looking Obi-Wan had deactivated his own lightsaber. With his arms extended at his sides, Obi-Wan looked like a hopeless clod. Maul grinned.

They don't know the power of the dark side. But they will . . . when I slay them.

Minutes passed. And then the laser doors opened.

Maul and Qui-Gon activated their lightsabers at the same time. Qui-Gon sprang forward, Maul moved backward, and the fight resumed. Behind Qui-Gon, Obi-Wan raced up through the security hallway, but he had to stop fast when the sixth laser door activated, cutting him off from Qui-Gon.

Warding off Qui-Gon's attack with each backward step, Maul maneuvered around the circular mouth of the generator's core, a virtually fathomless pit. Maul sensed

Qui-Gon was fighting without hatred, just as he sensed Obi-Wan's helplessness from behind the transparent laser door. He spun his lightsaber to deflect a rapid series of strikes from Qui-Gon's blade, then brought his own lightsaber up fast and slammed the side of its pommel against Qui-Gon's face, stunning the Jedi. And then, with a flick of his wrist, he drove one of his red blades straight through Qui-Gon's chest.

"No!"

The echoing shout came from Obi-Wan, who was still trapped behind the sixth laser door. Maul yanked the lightsaber free from Qui-Gon's torso and the Jedi collapsed beside the core.

Turning his back to Qui-Gon, Maul fixed his gaze on Obi-Wan. He deactivated his lightsaber and began pacing before the laser door, watching Obi-Wan as he waited for the door to open. He bared his teeth hungrily.

You're next.

When the door opened, Obi-Wan's lightsaber was blazing and so was Maul's. The young Jedi practically flew toward Maul. Their lightsabers smashed into each other. Maul spun and turned, flipping his lightsaber and forcing Obi-Wan to move that much faster with his inferior single-bladed weapon. Maul noticed that Obi-Wan was fighting more offensively than Qui-Gon, but it didn't matter. The boy would suffer the same fate as—

Obi-Wan's lightsaber came up fast and swept through the pommel of Maul's weapon. One half of

Maul's lightsaber shattered, leaving his left hand clutching what amounted to a still-functional single blade. Before he could react, Obi-Wan kicked him in the chest and he was sent sprawling onto his back near the edge of the core.

Obi-Wan leaped over Maul and tried to drive his lightsaber through Maul's prone body, but Maul blocked the strike and flung himself up from the floor. Obi-Wan landed behind Maul, but Maul turned and blocked another series of strikes before he kicked Obi-Wan in the jaw.

The Jedi moved with the kick, letting it carry him into a backflip. Landing on his feet, he struck back at Maul, driving them both away from the core. Maul flipped to the side and then used the power of the Force to shove Obi-Wan backward. Obi-Wan lost his grip on his lightsaber as he hit the floor. The lightsaber was still bouncing across the floor as he fell into the core.

Obi-Wan's lightsaber came to a stop. Maul grinned as he walked toward the weapon and then kicked it into the core. He leaned over the edge of the core to watch the lightsaber fall down the apparently bottomless hole. The lightsaber fell past Obi-Wan, who had managed to grab hold of a nub that jutted out from the core's upper wall, about two meters below the floor level.

Maul glared at Obi-Wan. He wondered how long the Jedi could cling to the nub. He knew Obi-Wan's hands and arms would get tired eventually. Growing impatient, Maul swung his pared-down lightsaber against the metal edge of the core's upper rim, sending sparks flying out over Obi-Wan's head. Maul noted that his blade did not damage the metal and realized it was impervious to energy weapons. He wondered if the metal could be crafted into body armor.

And then he noticed Obi-Wan was not looking up at him. The Jedi was staring at something along the core's upper wall. Or was he looking at something beyond the wall? Baffled by what the Jedi might be attempting, Maul scrunched his face angrily.

Obi-Wan flew up out of the core. Maul had forgotten about Qui-Gon Jinn's lightsaber, which flew up from the floor near the fallen Jedi's body and landed in the waiting hand of the still-airborne Obi-Wan.

Maul rapidly transferred his lightsaber from his right hand to his left. Obi-Wan activated Qui-Gon's lightsaber as he soared overhead and landed behind Maul. Maul spun fast, but not fast enough to stop Obi-Wan from swinging Qui-Gon's blade through his midsection.

Maul grunted involuntarily as every nerve in his body went into shock. His vision blurred and he blinked his eyes, trying to regain his focus. He wanted to fight back. He wanted to slay Obi-Wan, but his body would not obey him. Obi-Wan slid out of his range of vision, and then Maul saw the chamber's ceiling. He realized he was falling backward into the core.

No.

And as he fell, the upper half of his body separated from the lower.

No.

As his remains tumbled down the generator shaft, he kept his eyes open and fought to remain conscious. But then his head struck the shaft's wall, and everything went dark.

No!

His mind screamed. Despite everything he had learned about death and duty from his Master, Maul knew he was not yet ready to die. Not after so many years of training, and with so much more to accomplish. Not so long as he still had so much hatred within him.

Obi-Wan ruined me!

He willed himself to see. A moment later, his vision returned. The shaft's walls were a disorienting blur. Across the shaft he sighted his own black-clad legs, scissoring lifelessly at the air as they fell. He struggled to right his torso so he could see downward.

Can't die!

He fell past an oval shadow, and then a similar shadow raced by, along with a whooshing sound.

Air vents.

Maul hoped that there was at least one more vent below, that it would be large enough to accommodate his diminished body. He extended his arms, and his left hand's fingertips suddenly burned with friction as they brushed against the cylindrical wall.

Must live!

Hoping, wishing, praying for one more air vent . . .

Must kill Obi-Wan!

. . . he reached out with the Force.

CHAPTER EIGHTEEN

"Far above . . . far above . . . we don't know where we'll fall," muttered the creature as he used a broken bit of blackened bone to scratch a drawing onto the wall of his cavernous dwelling, his bare back warmed by the small fire he'd built. "Far above . . . what once was great is rendered small." The drawing consisted of a pair of small silhouettes, a man's upper body separated from his lower body, each half apparently descending between two vertical lines that indicated a deep chute.

The creature sighed. "Nowhere to go but down."

More than a decade had passed since the skirmish that had become known as the Battle of Naboo. The creature that had once been Darth Maul moved on his spiderlike droid legs through a tunnel on the planet Lotho Minor. He still didn't know how long he'd been in the tunnel, or how or when he'd arrived on such a dismal world. He still remembered nothing about his life before, when he lived aboveground. All he had left were his anger and his hunger.

"Falling, falling, falling." He looked at his other drawings of small figures on the wall. Some figures were being tortured, others killed. Many were fighting with burning sticks. Some sticks were blue. Some were red. The creature liked the red sticks.

No, not sticks. Sticks are wrong. Something else that cuts and burns like . . .

He heard something move in the upper levels, a slithering sound that he recognized as coming from the one who called himself Morley. Morley was a snakelike scavenger who should have kept his distance. *Stupid Morley.*

And then he heard footsteps. Someone was walking with Morley.

Someone very big. On two legs.

Lowering the bone he'd been using as a drawing stick, he kept to the shadows as he scurried up a wall, careful not to make a sound. Despite his damaged memories, he knew every crevice and foothold in the tunnels.

As he shifted his metal legs up toward the ceiling, he looked down and saw Morley's shadowy form slink into the dark chamber. Near Morley, another dark form shifted, a hulking humanoid. A small point of light radiated and moved across the area of the big man's chest.

Something glowing, something burns . . .

"He's going to get you!" Morley cried.

The big man spun around and moved away from Morley. Morley shouted, "He's going to eat you alive!"

The creature clinging to the ceiling did not know whether Morley was threatening him or encouraging him to make a feast of the big man. The creature didn't care. He descended fast and pounced on Morley.

"No!" Morley screamed. "Not me! Please, not me!"

The creature squeezed Morley's writhing body. He liked the sounds of Morley's screams and desperate gasps for breath, but not as much as he enjoyed the loud snapping of bones as he broke Morley's spine.

Now for the big man.

The creature spotted something glowing in the darkness, recognized it as the point of light he'd seen on the other intruder's chest. He lurched forward on his metal legs and was about to spring when the man ignited a long red stick.

Not a stick.

A red blade made of pure energy. It was familiar. . . .
Mine!

The creature *knew* he had once owned the weapon, or one very much like it. He glared at the intruder, saw that the point of light against his chest was a small amulet that hung from a chain around his neck. The man's head was illuminated by the glowing red blade. His strong face was tattooed with jagged patterns, and horns extended from his skull.

A reflection?!

For unknown reasons, the creature thought of a boy floating outside a window.

Me? No! Not me!

Confused and outraged, the creature shrieked and launched himself at the intruder, slamming him against the wall. He grabbed for the weapon's handle but the intruder knocked him back. His six metal legs clattered as he tumbled across the floor, but he rolled up onto his tapered feet and lashed out again, punching and kicking. His fingers struck armor and powerful muscles. He barely noticed that the intruder was only trying to ward him off with the red blade, not strike him down.

He pried at the central grip, trying to yank the weapon from the intruder's grasp. He did not assume that the weapon housed separate components for each blade, his shattered mind not even comprehending the incredible technology. He just knew that it was familiar and deadly, and that he wanted it.

The weapon snapped in two, leaving the intruder holding one red blade and the creature with the other. And then they were fighting, the two blades clashing in the darkness. Their fight carried them through the cave, but then the intruder grunted and fell back.

"You, Darth Maul," the intruder said, "are who I've been searching for."

Darth Maul?

"I thought you were dead. You are my kin."

Memories flickered in the creature's mind . . . in *Maul's* mind. He growled. "No!"

"We are brothers."

Maul shook his head. "You don't know," Maul snapped. "You don't know anything!"

The intruder placed his hand over his chest. "I know I am your blood."

Maul glared at the intruder. *I don't know you!* He tried to read the stranger's expression. *Sorry for me? Disgusted?* Maul's blood began to boil. The stranger was nothing to him, not even a threat. Sneering, he cast aside the weapon and retreated into the cave.

He clambered over junk and shoved aside rotting carcasses, making his way back to the fire he'd built. It was still burning. He crouched on the filthy floor, stared at the drawings on the walls, and began chanting, "Never never never never never . . ."

The hulking stranger followed Maul to the fire. Looking around, the stranger said with dismay, "This is where you live?"

Without looking at the stranger, Maul nodded in response. He picked up a nearby bone and began gnawing on it.

The stranger noticed the weird and violent drawings that decorated the walls. "How long have you lived here?"

Maul nipped at the bone, his eyes rolling back and

forth madly as he replied, "Years and years and years and years."

"You are a powerful Sith," the stranger said solemnly. "The whole galaxy shook before your power. Do you remember?"

The whole galaxy?! Maul leered. "Always remember, always remember."

The stranger eyed the robotic apparatus beneath Maul's rib cage and said, "Your legs?"

"That scum took it," Maul said.

The stranger seemed pleased by Maul's answer. "The Jedi . . . you remember." Taking a cautious step toward Maul, the stranger said, "I've brought a gift for you."

"For me?" Maul said with disbelief. "Food?"

"No. Something to regain your memory." He removed the glowing talisman from his neck and handed it to Maul.

Maul clutched at the talisman. Rocking back and forth on his robot legs, he began chanting.

The stranger leaned closer to Maul. "Brother, what are you saying?"

But Maul wasn't listening. His focus was on the talisman, which glowed increasingly brighter in his hand. And then his mind was flooded by fragmented memories.

My childhood . . . my training . . . my Master!

In his mind, he saw a young man.

Scum!

The man was a Jedi.

Jedi scum! What's his name?

He knew the man's name was Obi-Wan Kenobi.

Maul's eyes went wide. And then he collapsed.

EPILOGUE

good Team wins

The hulking man claimed his name was Savage Opress. Like Maul, he was a Zabrak. According to Opress, Talzin had transformed him into a monstrous warrior, endowed him with dark side powers, and given him the amulet and sent him in search of Maul. Maul had no recollection of the amulet, the talisman Talzin had brushed against his bloodied arm years earlier. He didn't remember anyone named Talzin.

When Opress's starship left the planet Lotho Minor, Maul was with him. Opress had plotted a course for Dathomir. He explained that they would find Talzin on Dathomir, that Talzin would help Maul. Maul didn't know why Talzin would help him, but he did know that he needed help.

Because now he knew the identity of the person who had transformed him into a monster. He knew the man was a Jedi named Obi-Wan Kenobi. If Opress and Talzin could help Maul, they might help him find Kenobi. But

Maul also knew he was in bad shape, that what he could really use was a new set of legs.

And then he would make Kenobi pay.

He looked at Opress, who was seated behind the controls of the starship that was carrying them to the hyperspace jump point that would take them to Dathomir. Maul was not certain that Opress was his ally, let alone his brother. But Maul was willing to take a chance.

Maybe he's a reflection . . . maybe he's the boy outside the window.

Maul could only imagine what the future held, or whether he could trust the man who was bringing him to Dathomir. He hoped Opress was indeed his friend.

Everyone else could burn.

to Be cuntinyod

ACKNOWLEDGMENTS

Star Wars: The Wrath of Darth Maul reveals many new details about Darth Maul's life but also draws dialogue and situations from previously published books, including the screenplay for *Star Wars*: Episode I *The Phantom Menace* by George Lucas; the movie novelization of *Star Wars*: Episode I *The Phantom Menace* by Terry Brooks; and most notably *Star Wars*: Episode I *Journal — Darth Maul* by Jude Watson, which provided a wealth of information about Maul's childhood and training. I borrowed from Watson's book liberally and with great respect. The story also incorporates details from the television series *Star Wars: The Clone Wars* episode "Brothers," scripted by Katie Lucas.

I'm extremely grateful to writer James Luceno, who generously gave me some great ideas so *The Wrath of Darth Maul* would mesh with his novel *Darth Plagueis*, and also provided an early draft of his short story "Restraint," from which I also borrowed liberally; I

215

encourage readers to read "Restraint" for a more expansive account of Maul's exploits on the planet Orsis. Thanks also to former Scholastic editor Annmarie Nye for enlisting me to write this book; to editor Frank Parisi and Lucas Books executive editor Jonathan Rinzler for their valued input; and to Lucasfilm's Leland Chee for helping us *Star Wars* writers maintain continuity. Thanks to Greg Mitchell for reminding me about the *Dusty Duck*. And thanks to my daughter Violet for reading an advance version of this book's early chapters and reassuring me I could make at least one person feel sorry for Darth Maul.